MURDER AT MACKLYN COVE

Book Five In The
O'Toole/Starker
Murder Mystery Series

G. A. Cockerham

ISBN-13: 978-1-7339973-4-8

Acclaim for G. A. Cockerham's mysteries

—Featured in Who's Who/What's What Book Picks
in *Southern Oregon* Magazine.

Amazon Reviews:

Murder On The Oregon Coast

—Quick-paced writing with strong characters and good detail of police procedures. The setting is authentic and gives insight into the beauty and charm of small-town Brookings and its environs.

—Police procedural in a small town detective story with brilliant deductive work.

Murder On The Wind

—Excellent detail of police procedure, as well as insight into the state and federal law enforcement agencies… A nice bonus is the historical background of several locations in the book.

Murder Replete…*for now*

—Meticulous descriptions of police procedure…accurate depictions of the local geography and culture.

—I just finished reading 1-3 of this series, and all I have to say is wow!

Murder Takes All

—I have read all the O'Toole/Starker Murder Mystery Series. This was a "could not put down" book.

—Great book! … written with interesting twists, turns and surprises

—knowledge of local history and geography, as well as forensic detail, are on display throughout.

Also by G. A. Cockerham

O'TOOLE/STARKER
OREGON COAST MURDER MYSTERIES

Murder On The Oregon Coast

Murder On The Wind

Murder Replete...*for now*

Murder Takes All

ACKNOWLEDGEMENTS

Listed below are the names of several people whose expertise contributed greatly to the authenticity and human-interest aspects of my mystery by providing input based upon personal experience. To each I give my gratitude.

My husband, Bruce Cockerham, edits my law enforcement references and is my constant source of support and encouragement. Bruce is a retired police captain with thirty years of experience in law enforcement. He's worked in patrol, traffic, detectives, SWAT, administration, and as an academy instructor. Bruce trained with the FBI as a counter sniper and is a graduate of both the California Command College and the FBI National Academy. He holds a BA from Whitworth University and an MDiv from the San Francisco Theological Seminary.

Forensic DNA expert Camilla Green provides me with little-known forensic techniques. Cami's expertise has placed her in several television shows including *Cold Justice*, *Cold Justice: Sex Crimes*, *On the Case with Paula Zahn*, and *Murder Decoded*.

Ted Heath retired after thirty-three years with the Curry County Sheriff's Office. He served as a member of the Sheriff's Search and Rescue (SAR) team throughout his law enforcement career and has continued to be an active SAR member since retirement. Ted's years in law enforcement included ten years on patrol and twenty years in the Marine Division where he was responsible for enforcing boating regulations. Ted participated in numerous SAR missions on the Rogue River and in the Pacific Ocean. His expertise has resulted in locating many missing persons, both alive and deceased. He was given charge of the SAR program for the last six years of his career and was subsequently promoted to Sergeant in charge of SAR and Marine and Forest Patrol.

Logan Couch has served for twenty years as a member of the Curry County Sheriff's Office Search and Rescue (SAR) team. He has served in many capacities including that of Training Facilitator, Search Manager, Safety Officer, Public Information Officer, and Incident Command. He is certified for all SAR teams and is a certified swimmer and snow-tracker. Logan has been recognized by several agencies for his SAR efforts and the lives he helped save.

Hugh Holden has actively SCUBA and freedived since the early '70's. His diving has taken him up and down the Pacific coast from Puget Sound to Costa Rica, to the Hawaiian Islands, and many islands and lakes in the Caribbean. He's harvested abalone and spearfished, primarily in California waters.

TABLE OF CONTENTS

CHAPTER ONE

"You know we'll be arrested and fined if we're caught."

Max adjusted his tank, took hold of one of the hose regulators, and checked that the pressure gauge was working.

"You agreed to join us, Jerry. We've had this planned for weeks. Feeling something akin to buyer's remorse?"

Jerry exhaled slowly before responding. "No problem."

Max took in air from his regulator, testing it. "Let's go over our plan once more."

Stuart glanced at his watch. "Better make it quick. The fog's not going to sit offshore for much longer. It'll be great cover for us coming out of the water with abalone, but it will also delay our getting out of the harbor if we don't leave soon."

Max agreed. "Okay. I'll make it quick. We'll drop anchor at Diver Rock, stay down for forty-five minutes, and then surface with our catch. Stuart parked his car this morning at the Macklyn Cove Mill Beach parking lot. You two can swim to shore with your catch and mine, put them in the trunk of the car, and meet me at my place about seven. That will give you time to change out of your wet suits and then prepare our abalone. I'll take the boat back to the harbor and head home. Any questions?"

Max looked at Jerry who shook his head. Stuart sat quietly. "New wet suit, Stu?"

"Yeah. Got it last week. It's 6mm. Not as good as a dry suit but a lot warmer than what I'd been wearing."

Max laughed. "It's warmer because it doesn't have a hole in it like that old second-hand thing you were wearing." He looked at Jerry. "Word to the wise. Don't use second-hand equipment for diving."

Stuart ignored the dig. "Let's just go."

The three guys stepped into the boat, and Max started the engine, crossed the bar, and headed north.

They were moving at a good pace when Stuart noticed Jerry staring at the bottom of the boat and sitting with his arms crossed across his stomach. "Hey, Jerry, you going to be sick?"

Jerry looked up. "No. Just thinking."

Stuart glanced at Max and Max toward Jerry.

"Thinking about what?" Max asked.

"I haven't dived for a few years and never really got certified. How deep will we be diving?"

"It's about twenty-five feet near the rock where we'll anchor," said Max. "You good for that?"

"Yeah. Twenty-five feet won't be a problem. I should be able to make that without the tank if anything goes wrong."

Max smiled. "A problem? You won't have a problem if you stick to the plan. Just dive down, pry off a few abalone and come back up within forty-five minutes." Max paused to let Jerry speak up if he had any more concerns.

Jerry spoke hesitantly. "It's just that we can't get caught. I heard there's a huge penalty for poaching abalone. We could even go to jail."

Max glanced at Stuart and nodded his head toward Jerry as though asking Stuart to participate in the conversation.

Stuart responded. "Well, we're not going to get caught. We stick to the plan and a few hours from now we'll be drinking beer and enjoying our harvest shucked, gutted, sliced into fine steaks, and fried to a golden brown."

Jerry unfolded his arms and smiled. "I'm looking forward to it, and I'll bet twenty right now that I bring in the highest count."

"You're on," said Stuart and Max simultaneously.

Max slowed the boat down to a stop and threw over the anchor. "We're here. It's four-fifteen. We'll all come back up no later than five. Stu can go in first and move to the right around the back of the rock. I'll go over a couple of safety features with Jerry before we go in."

Stuart fitted his mouthpiece and rolled backward into the water. Max had Jerry sit on the side of the boat.

"Before you go in, let's go over a couple of rules," said Max. "It's been a while since you've dived, so I want you to stay close to me. There's a lot of kelp in this area, which is why we should find a mess of abalone. But kelp can be dangerous. I've got my knife in the event either of us gets our tank caught up in it. When you're ready to return to the boat, swim over to me and let me know. We'll go up together, slowly. You won't need to worry about narcosis, or the three-martini effect, but divers have experienced the bends even in shallow water when they've surfaced too quickly."

"Three martinis?" asked Jerry.

"Yeah. Divers say that for every thirty feet down, you feel as though you've drunk a martini."

Jerry nodded. "Okay. Like I said before, twenty-five feet shouldn't be a problem. Stuart has a head start on us, and I'm eager to get in the water. All right if I go now?"

"Sure," said Max. "I'll be in right after you."

Jerry inserted his mouthpiece, started to roll backwards, and hesitated. He quickly lifted his arm toward the mouthpiece again.

Max gave Jerry a hard push and followed. Once in the water, Max looked around and couldn't see Stuart. He looked to his left and saw Jerry begin to go limp. Max pulled out Jerry's mouthpiece and pushed him further to the left of the rock and into a bed of seaweed. He took hold of Jerry's hand for a few seconds, then swam around and pried a few abalone off the rocks. He waited until he'd been down about forty-five minutes, then surfaced. Stuart was in the boat with his catch. "How many?" Max asked, looking at Stuart's bag.

"Six. Could have pried off more if I didn't have to come up. What about you?"

"Three," said Max. "I lost time giving Jerry a few last-minute safety tips."

Stuart looked toward the rock. "Did you see him down there?"

Max shook his head in the negative. "He went in first and took off before I got in."

"I'm surprised," said Stuart, "that he made this trip. He said he's never been certified, and it sounded like he hasn't done much diving. I know you said the two of you were in high school together, but how did you get in touch for this dive?"

"I ran into him a month ago in Cave Junction. I was on my way back from Medford and stopped at Taylor's. I was eating lunch when Jerry came up to me and asked if I was Max Rainy. We got to talking, I told him about our dives, and he said he'd like to join us."

Stuart nodded. "And he knew diving for abalone is illegal in Oregon?"

"Yeah. He knew. Talked enough for me to know that it wouldn't be his first offense."

Stuart looked at his watch. "It's five-ten. Seems he's not only inexperienced but late too."

Max looked across the water. "Maybe I'd better go down and get him. Can you handle swimming to shore with your bag and mine too?"

"Yeah. I won't need a tank, so I'll leave my vest with you." He nodded toward his abalone bag. "I want to get these into my trunk before the fog dissipates. What will you do with Jerry's catch when he comes up?"

"I'll take care of it," said Max. "Oh, by the way. I asked a friend to meet you on shore to help get the abalone to the car. His name's Peter. Bring him back to the house with you."

"A friend? You didn't say anything about another friend helping. First Jerry, now Peter. That's two more people who know we're poaching abalone."

"Don't worry, Stu. I can assure you that Peter won't talk. Just as I know that you'll never talk."

Stuart shook his head. "Well, I don't like it."

Stuart entered the water. Max handed him the bags of abalone.

"See you about seven," Max yelled. He fell back into the water and held onto the side of the boat. Twenty minutes later he climbed back in, started the engine, and headed toward the harbor.

CHAPTER TWO

The fog had lifted to reveal a beautiful fall day on the coast. Unlike other areas of the country, the southern Oregon coast doesn't experience four distinct seasons. The effect of the ocean on the atmosphere keeps temperatures moderate year-round with few exceptions. The temperature on this day was a comfortable sixty-one degrees with winds at three miles per hour.

Detective Patty O'Toole was at her desk when the call came through.

"Is he here now? Okay, put him in the interview room. Starker and I will be there in a minute." She ended the call as Detective Rick Starker walked into the room with a plate.

"It's Sally's birthday cake. Chocolate with raspberry filling. You might want to get a piece now before Brad and Pete discover it."

Patty stood up from her desk and grabbed her jacket from the back of her chair.

"I'll have to risk losing out, and you'll have to save yours for later. The front desk just called. There's a Randy Stengle in the interview room who thinks his brother may have been murdered."

Rick took the fork out of his mouth, put it down with his plate, and put his jacket on. "I'm going to need coffee soon after a couple bites of this cake. You want a cup?"

"No, I'll pass."

The detectives walked down the hall to the interview room. Though a department with more resources might have a soft interview room for purposes other than interrogating suspects, this one was also used for interrogations. The only thing on the four walls was a one-way mirror.

Mr. Stengle sat at the table facing the wall with the mirror.

The detectives walked in. Patty sat down opposite Stengle while Rick remained at the door. She made the introduction.

"I'm Detective O'Toole and this is Detective Starker."

Rick motioned toward the door. "I was about to get a cup of coffee, Mr. Stengle. Can I bring you one too?"

Stengle nodded. "Sure."

Rick was gone for twenty seconds before he returned and took a seat next to Patty. "Officer Bradley is getting our coffees," he said while removing a small pad and pen from his shirt pocket. He leaned back in his chair.

Patty opened the conversation. "The front office told us you're here about your brother. You think he's been murdered?"

Stengle nodded. "That's right. Jerry and I share a house in Cave Junction. We let each other know if we're going to be gone for more than a couple of nights. Jerry left five days ago, and I've not heard from him since."

Rick took notes while Patty continued. "Does Jerry have a girlfriend?"

"No. Not now. He broke up with his last girlfriend a few months ago."

"Has Jerry stayed away from home before without letting you know?"

"No, Detective. He hasn't."

Rick lowered his pen. "You seem awfully sure about that."

"Let me explain. Cave Junction has the reputation of being like the 'Old West', when a sheriff didn't have enough deputies to keep law abiding citizens safe. We lost our parents about twelve years ago. They left for a week-long, well-deserved vacation. When eight days passed without hearing from them, we called the police and learned that they'd been kidnapped only a few miles out of town, then murdered.

"Jerry was eighteen at the time. I was fifteen. We promised each other after that to let the other know if we were going to spend more than a couple of days away from home."

Patty paused. "And how long has it been since you've seen Jerry?"

"Five days."

"Why do you think he's been murdered and not just been delayed due to an accident or new girlfriend?"

"Well, like I said, if he were delayed for some reason, he'd have sent me a text. I've not seen anything on the news nor heard about an accident. But there's another reason. He left here to go diving with some guy and was planning to be back that evening."

"So maybe he did go diving, and they decided to take more dive trips up the coast."

Stengle shook his head. "You're not hearing me. Jerry would have let me know what he was doing. We're brothers and best buddies. He'd have known I'd be worried. I didn't like the idea of him going diving with that Brookings guy."

"Why's that?" Patty asked.

Stengle looked down at the table. "Because Jerry isn't certified, and he hasn't dived for two or three years. I asked if he let this other guy know that he wasn't certified, and he said yes." Stengle looked puzzled as he spoke. "If the guy from Brookings is a responsible, certified diver, why would he be willing to take Jerry on the trip?"

Patty leaned back in the chair and glanced at Rick.

Rick sat forward. "What's the name of the guy from Brookings?"

"His first name is Max. Jerry didn't mention his last name."

"How did your brother and Max meet up?"

"Jerry told me he ran into Max at Taylor's. Max recognized Jerry from high school and approached him. They shot the breeze for a bit, and then Max invited Jerry on this dive trip."

"Do you know what they were diving for?"

The worried man slouched down in the chair. "That's another problem."

The detectives glanced at each other.

"Jerry said they were going to dive for abalone."

Patty raised her eyebrows. "But that's currently illegal."

"I know, and I said so to Jerry."

Rick made a note in his pad. "What did Jerry say?"

"He told me that he'd be careful. That Max knew exactly where they could dive with little chance of being seen. And no chance of being seen if the fog rolls in."

Patty leaned forward in her chair and made sure she had Stengle's attention.

"How long was your brother in for?"

The question made Stengle fidget as he pushed his hands against the table, rocking onto the two back legs of his metal chair. "Why are you asking me that?"

"Because Jerry agreed to go with Max for the purpose of doing something unlawful. So either your brother is ignorant or he's not foreign to the consequences of breaking the law."

Stengle looked around the room. "Okay, you're right. But our parents' deaths really messed him up for a while. Shortly after their deaths, Jerry was in a serious accident. Then he did time for stealing a couple of cars." The room became silent as Stengle recovered his composure.

"My brother isn't a bad guy, Detectives. The thing is, I think Max is. I think something's happened to my brother."

Rick looked up from his notes and glanced at Patty.

She turned her attention back to Stengle. "We'll need Max's last name. Do you know if your brother has a high school yearbook? If not, we'll need to know the name of his high school and the years he attended. I also want you to write down the make, color, and license plate of Jerry's car. And the time of day and date that you last saw him."

Stengle let out a sigh and sank into his chair. "So you'll look for him?"

"We'll see what we can do," said Patty. "Give all the information we've requested to Officer Bradley."

Patty and Rick stood up, and Rick gave the young man his business card. "Call if your brother returns home or if you think of anything else that might be helpful."

The detectives stepped out of the room, and Patty briefed Officer "Brad"

Bradley on what they requested. He picked up a pad and pen from the front desk and walked down the hall to talk with Stengle.

At their desks, Rick proceeded to eat his cake and drink his now-cold coffee. Patty stared out of the only window in the office.

"What do you make of that?"

Rick swallowed and put his plate down. "I think he's telling the truth. The question is whether his brother is alive and well and just hasn't checked in, or he found himself in the company of some bad dudes and is lying in a ditch somewhere. We'll know more after talking with Max. What are your thoughts? Do you think he's telling the truth?"

"I do and, like you said, we need to know more. Once we have Max's last name, we may find a mug shot that we can show down at the port. If they were poaching abalone, it's possible someone saw them getting off the boat with their catch."

Rick nodded. "I'll write up the report if you want to follow up with Brad."

Patty nodded. "Works for me." She sat back in her chair. "I guess this could be our first official murder investigation since your return to Brookings. Still glad to be back?"

Rick smiled. "Yeah. My going to work for the Justice Department was the right thing to do at the time. My life was complicated, and I needed time to figure out what I wanted to do. Being a special agent was a good experience. It exposed me to another level of law enforcement I'd not previously known. But I missed the rural lifestyle we have here on the coast, and I missed my friends."

Rick looked into Patty's eyes. She returned his glance. When the pause in the conversation went on a little too long, she stood up.

"I'll go talk with Brad."

Before leaving her desk, Patty's cell phone lit up. "It's Mom," she said out loud and then answered. "Detective O'Toole."

"Well, hello, Detective O'Toole. How's your morning going?"

"It's okay, Mom. How's yours?"

"Mine is okay too. Bill is sleeping. He woke up about three this morning, got up for a while, and made himself a snack. He came back to bed about five and will probably sleep another hour. This has been his routine lately."

"Does Bill like his routine, Mom? And what about you? It seems like it would interfere with your ability to get a good night's rest."

"I think it's okay with him. As for me, I just go back to sleep."

"Well, Mom, seems the two of you have it worked out. What have you got planned for the day?"

"I'm going to work in the yard. This last storm made a mess of things. Bill will probably help where he can, but he's more inclined to sit and read nowadays."

"Has he had his hearing checked yet?'

"No, he hasn't. He doesn't see the need." Maggie laughed. "Conversations with him are becoming quite comical. You should have heard us yesterday."

"I've got time, Mom, and could use a laugh. Tell me about it."

Maggie laughed again. "I don't remember exactly but it went something like this. You need to know, first, that this was shortly before lunch time, and Bill was hungry. So I asked if he'd heard about Sue, and Bill asked me, 'What kind of soup?' So I asked if he was thinking about lunch."

"He said, 'A hunch? Why are you asking me if I have a hunch?'"

Patty laughed. "I take it that wasn't the end of your conversation."

"I was ready for it to end, so I told Bill to forget I said anything. Then I told him that I was going to call Tom and Sue. And…." Maggie laughed again. "Bill asked, 'Tiramisu? I love Tiramisu. Now that I know we're having dessert, I won't have a second bowl of soup.'"

"Oh, Mom. Though it's funny, it does seem that Bill seriously needs hearing aids."

"I know, dear. And I'm going to gently get him there. So far, his hearing hasn't affected his weekly get-together with his guy friends. Maybe I'll talk to Tom about coaching Bill toward accepting that he needs help."

"That's a good idea, Mom. Changing the subject, does Bill miss his gambling?"

"I've asked him about that, Patty. He says that he doesn't. You know, Bill has a saying. 'There's a season for everything,' and he's accepted that his season as a professional gambler is over."

"That's a good way for all of us to look at life, Mom. I'm glad the two of you have each other during this season of your lives."

"I am too, dear. Well, I hear him getting up, so I'll let you go. Have a good day and stay safe out there."

"I will, Mom. Hope the day goes well for you and Bill, too."

Rick looked up when Patty set down her cell phone. "Judging by your laughter, your mom and Bill seem to be doing okay."

"Yeah. They are. His hearing is gone. That creates some funny conversations. Mom is going to ask a friend of theirs to help convince Bill he needs hearing aids."

"I wonder why his hearing's so bad. Was he a shooter?"

"No, I don't think so. But he is eighty-eight, and that alone can be what's wrong with his hearing."

"I guess I'd forgotten that he's much older than your mom."

Patty nodded. "I didn't like the idea at first of her dating a man so much older, but he's been great for her. Because of Bill, Mom's been on cruises around the world. He's also been kind to her, and kindness counts for a lot."

"I agree," said Rick. "They're lucky."

Patty noticed Officer Bradley standing by the door of the detectives' office. "Hey, Brad. You got something for us?"

"Yeah. I called the high school attended by Max, the friend of the guy who's gone missing. His last name's Rainy. So I ran him through the system. He was arrested eight years ago for stealing cars from a used-car lot. A Ford and a Dodge. Here's his address."

Rick stood up, took the sheet of paper from Brad, and read off the address.

"Let's go talk to this guy," said Patty as she stood and put her jacket on.

Rick felt for his gun and grabbed his windbreaker before they both walked out the door.

Patty buckled her seat belt and took another look at the address. "He's in the trailer park just north of town."

Rick turned onto Highway 101, known through Brookings as Chetco Avenue. "I know the park. I don't recognize his name, which makes me wonder how long he's lived there."

"Patrol would know. By the way, I've been meaning to ask if you've been down to the harbor yet to see the new Lucy Dick statue across from the mouth of the river?"

Rick nodded as two lanes merged into one. "The Chetco tribe did a great job on the replica village. I guess she was the last full-blooded Chetco Indian when she moved back to the Chetco Valley to live out her life. I'll bet you know more about her and the tribe."

"I do. I've read there were only about a thousand Indians in the Chetco tribe and yet they were moved off the land and north to Siletz."

"Siletz?" asked Rick.

"It's a little more than two hundred miles north of here. Lucy died in 1940 and is buried at the Pioneer Cemetery in Harbor. Her descendants are enrolled members of the confederated Tribes of Siletz Indians in Oregon."

"I didn't know that," said Rick. "Who's responsible for the local project?"

"The Chetco Memorial project was established in 2009 by a group of Chetco Indian descendants. The goal was to design and construct a historical marker to commemorate the history of the Chetco Indian people. And what's really awesome is that the monument is built directly on top of the remains of a Chetco Indian village. The underground village was discovered in 2011 during repair work on areas damaged by our tsunami earlier that year."

"Underground village," Rick repeated. "That must have been quite a historical find."

"It turned out to be," said Patty. "They found numerous Indian artifacts making the site culturally significant on a grand scale."

Rick turned into the trailer park. "It's good that the site has been preserved. I'll get down to the harbor and take a closer look." He pointed ahead. "I'm guessing the trailer we want is up there on the right."

"That's it," Patty said. "The tan one with the lawn that needs mowing and the broken porch railing. Look familiar?"

Rick parallel-parked on the street in front of the trailer. "Not to me."

The detectives walked to the front door, and Rick knocked. A few seconds later, the door slowly opened. Both detectives showed their credentials.

Patty looked up at the young man standing at the door. He looked like he'd just woken up. His shirt was buttoned wrong, and he was in his socks.

"Are you Max Rainy?"

Seeing the detectives rendered the man momentarily speechless. With furrowed brows he responded in the negative.

"Can you get him?" Patty asked.

The young man left the door ajar, stepped back, and called for Max. A minute later, the door was opened again by another man who appeared to be in his mid-twenties. He too had not yet put his shoes on.

"What can I do for you, officers?"

"We're detectives," said Patty. "O'Toole and Starker. We'd like to ask you a few questions about a missing person's report we've received. May we come in?"

Max looked surprised and didn't move. "Missing person? I don't know anyone who's missing."

Rick stepped up to the top of the three steps in front of the door. "It's just a few questions. Mind if we come in?"

Max paused and then opened the door. With a puzzled look on his face, he let the detectives in. "Sure, come on in. Please excuse the mess." Max cleared a few pieces of clothing off the couch to make room for the detectives. He handed the pile of clothes to the other man, who stood with his back against the wall.

"What do you want to ask me?"

Patty and Rick remained standing. Rick took a small pad and pen from his pocket. Patty looked around the room and then at Max. "Is your name Max Rainy?"

Max nodded. "Yeah, that's right."

"Do you have a fishing boat?"

"Well, it's not a boat rigged for fishing, but I do have a small boat."

Rick continued to write while Patty asked questions.

"What do you use it for?"

Max sat down on the couch and leaned forward. "Diving mostly." He gestured toward the man standing against the wall. "My friend Stuart and I dive together now and then. That's why you see some of our gear on the kitchen table. We went out a few days ago."

Patty glanced at Rick as he walked toward the kitchen. "Mind if Detective Starker takes a look at your equipment?"

Max quickly looked up at Stuart. "Uh, I guess that would be okay. It's just diving stuff. Stuart can answer any questions about what's there."

Stuart followed Rick into the kitchen as Patty resumed her questioning. "When was that?"

Max looked back to Patty. "Huh?

"You said you went diving a few days ago. On what day?"

"Well, today is Wednesday, so it must have been Sunday."

"Just the two of you?"

"It's always just us," said Max. "Nobody else we know in Brookings dives."

"Where did you dive?"

Max looked down at his hands again. "We have a lot of dive spots up the coast. It always just depends upon the weather and how far we want to travel."

"I see," said Patty. "Where did you dive last Sunday?"

Max hesitated before replying. "Oh, here in Brookings we go to Macklyn Cove."

Patty nodded. "Something special about Macklyn Cove?"

"Yeah. If I were going to walk in, Mill Beach at the cove is perfect. The surf is usually much calmer than some of the other beaches. And Zwag Island and Diver Rock are great spots for spearfishing."

Patty smiled. "I didn't know that. What were you diving for last Sunday?"

Max laughed. "Stu and I went spearfishing for rockfish. That's pretty much all we do around here." Max shifted on the couch. "You're asking a lot of questions, Detective. I thought you said you wanted to ask me about a missing person."

Rick and Stuart walked back into the living room where Stuart leaned up against the wall.

Rick stepped up next to Patty. Patty looked at Rick. Then back to Max.

"Do you know a Jerry Stengle?"

Max looked down at the floor and rubbed his forehead. "Hmm. I know that name, but I can't think of where I've heard it." Max looked across the room at Stuart. "Do you know him?"

Stuart shook his head.

Rick took the high school photo of Jerry out of his pocket and showed it to Max.

"According to Jerry's brother, you and Jerry were in high school together."

Max looked at the photo and threw his head back. "That's how I know the name. Yeah. I knew Jerry in school. Is he the one you think is missing?"

"When's the last time you saw him?" Patty asked.

Max repeated Patty's question. "When was the last time I saw Jerry? Well, I don't think I've seen him since high school. Not since we graduated. That was eight years ago."

Rick had his pen and pad in his hands again. "Why do you think Jerry's brother thinks Jerry recently went fishing with you?"

"Gee, Detective. I don't know why he'd say that. Like I said, I haven't seen Jerry since high school."

"That's all the questions we have now," said Patty. She and Rick turned toward the door.

"Wait a minute," said Max. "You know, we don't know other divers who live in Brookings, but there are a couple of guys out of Port Orford who come down to Brookings to dive. You might want to talk to them."

Rick pulled out his pad. "Do you know their names?"

Max nodded. "Just their first names. One is Trevor." He looked at Stuart. "What was that other guy's name?"

Stuart stared at the floor before answering. "Connor."

"That's right," said Max. "Trevor and Connor. They hang out at Griff's on the Dock."

Patty glanced at Rick and then turned her attention back to Max.

"Thanks for your time. We'll contact you both again if we have more questions."

Max looked at his dive partner before answering. "Sure. No problem."

Rick slid his pen and paper into his shirt pocket. He pulled out a couple of business cards and handed one each to Max and Stuart.

"Call if you think of anything that might help us."

Max took the card. "Sure."

Once back in their car, Patty asked Rick, "See anything interesting in the kitchen?"

"Several dive items on the table. I don't know much about the sport, but I recognized the masks, mouthpieces, and booties. There's something called an 'octopus' that Stuart explained to me. I asked about wet suits. He said his is at home, and that Max usually keeps his in the garage. We'll want a diver to accompany us if we need to search his place. What did you think of Max? Telling the truth?"

Patty took a deep breath and slowly exhaled. "It's hard to tell. He could have been telling the truth. But why would Jerry have told his brother that he was going fishing with Max?"

Rick started the engine. "I agree. It makes no sense. Do you want to drive up to Port Orford now?"

"I do, but I need to clear it first with the LT." Patty called and waited for the lieutenant to answer. "Hi, LT. Rick and I just finished talking with Max Rainy, the guy our missing fisherman was to have met up with before disappearing. Rainy says the meet-up never took place. He gave us the names of a couple of divers who hang out at Griff's in Port Orford. So Rick and I will drive up there and see what we can find on the two."

Rick drove while listening to Patty's side of the conversation.

"Okay," she said. "Sure. No problem. We're just leaving the trailer park. Thanks."

Patty ended the call and filled Rick in on the lieutenant's comments.

"We need to go back to the office and pick up a package the chief wants dropped off at Bandon PD. He was going to send Pete, but since we have to go as far as Port Orford anyway, we'll drive on to Bandon."

"Great," said Rick. "I saw on my phone weather app this morning that we should have twenty-five-foot waves today and tomorrow. I love driving this stretch of highway between Brookings and Port Orford when the big waves are crashing against our offshore sea stacks."

"Yeah," said Patty. "You know that I do too. I also love going into Winter

River Books in Bandon. You've probably not been there, have you? It's been Bandon's independent store since 1983."

Rick smiled as he turned into the police department driveway. "As a matter of fact, I have. I told you that I like giving books as gifts. While you pick up whatever the chief wants us to take to Bandon, I'm going to see if there are any cookies in the break room."

CHAPTER THREE

The detectives drove to Port Orford, a small coastal town about sixty miles north of Brookings. Rick drove out to the dock. They parked facing Griff's, a small seafood restaurant surrounded on three sides by commercial fishing boats and ocean.

"Hard to believe," said Patty, "that it's been six years since that building was severely damaged by the storm."

"The perfect storm," said Rick. "I remember the newspaper headlines. *High tide and waves just under thirty feet.* That combination created enough power for waves to crash over the jetty, removing several giant boulders and pulling a small structure into the sea. Luckily, no lives were lost."

Patty unbuckled her seat belt. "No lives lost, but a clear example of the power of the ocean, something many tourists don't understand. I hope we don't lose anyone this year." She turned to step out of the car. "Maybe these guys can shed some light on our missing diver."

The detectives walked into the lobby of the restaurant and waited for one of the servers.

"Sit anywhere you like," said a young woman with a full dinner plate in each hand.

Patty showed her badge. "We're here to ask a few questions. Is the owner around?'

The woman turned to deliver the meals. "I'll get her."

"Did you see the fish on that plate?" asked Rick.

"I did. And it was probably caught right out there."

A petite woman in her thirties walked up to the detectives. She wore an apron and had her long hair pulled back into a ponytail. She looked at Patty and Rick.

"You wanted to talk to me?"

Patty stepped forward. "We do. We've been told that we might find a couple of fishermen here by the names of Connor and Trevor. Do you know them?"

The woman laughed. "Yeah, I know them, but Conner and Trevor are not considered fishermen to a lot of the commercial guys around here. They're wannabes." She nodded toward the back of the room. "The corner table in back. You two want coffee or a piece of pie?"

Patty glanced at Rick, who looked ready to accept, and turned back to the owner. "No, thanks. We don't expect to be long."

Patty and Rick looked at the two guys sitting at the back table, and Patty whispered to Rick, "They look a bit like Mutt and Jeff. Definitely too old to be hanging out in the middle of the day."

Rick raised his eyebrows. "I wonder who's Mutt and who's Jeff?"

Patty started for their table. "Let's find out."

Patty and Rick approached the table, abruptly putting a halt to the conversation that the guys had been having.

"Connor?" Patty asked.

The taller of the two leaned back in his chair. "Who's asking?"

Both detectives showed their credentials. "I'm Detective O'Toole and this is Detective Starker. Are you Connor?"

Connor looked nervously at Trevor. "Yeah."

Rick took notes while Patty continued with the questioning. "And your last name?"

"Brown."

Patty looked at the shorter of the two. "You must be Trevor."

Trevor nodded. "Yeah. Why?"

Patty ignored his question. "Your last name?"

"Hartlyn. Trevor Hartlyn."

Patty took a photo of Jerry out of her pocket and placed it on the table in front of Connor.

"Have you seen him?"

Connor shook his head and moved the photo in front of Trevor.

Trevor looked at it and moved it back to Connor. "I don't know who he is."

"His name's Jerry Stengle," said Patty. "That mean anything to either of you?"

Connor put his fork down. "Why are you asking us about this guy?"

Patty ignored Connor's questions, returned the photo to her pocket, and looked up at him.

"What about Max Rainy?"

Max's name triggered a momentary reaction of recognition by both Connor and Trevor.

"Don't know him either," said Connor.

Patty looked at Rick and then back to Connor. "Well, that's not what Max told us. He's the one who told us we could find the two of you here."

Connor looked down at the table and then back at Patty. "Really? What's his name, again?"

"Max Rainy."

Connor looked at Trevor. "Is that the guy we met the last time we fished Pistol River?"

"Could be," said Trevor. "Yeah, I think his name was Max."

"Is this Max guy in some kind of trouble?" asked Connor.

"That's an interesting way to respond," said Patty. "Why do you ask?"

Connor sat back in his chair again and looked at Trevor. Trevor looked down at the table, leaving Connor to answer Patty's question.

"No reason," said Connor.

Patty glanced at Rick. He stepped around to the far side of the table.

"When's the last time you fished with Max?" Rick asked.

Connor paused before responding. "Well, let me think about that. Could have been last year sometime, maybe in the summer."

"Think again," said Rick. "Remember, we've already talked to Max."

Connor looked around the room. "It could have been a couple of months ago."

Rick made a note on his pad. "And where'd you fish?"

"Brookings' harbor, off the bank at the mouth of the Chetco."

"Why not use Max's boat?"

"That was our plan, but the fog was moving in and out that day. We decided to play it safe and stay off the water."

"Have you previously fished there with Max?"

Connor looked again at Trevor, and Trevor responded. "Just that one time, I think."

Rick looked back at Connor. "Other than the port, where do you two fish when you're in Brookings?"

"Zwag Island or Diver Rock."

Rick nodded. "Over at Macklyn Cove."

"Yeah."

"There's a nice beach there," said Rick. "You ever enter the water from Mill Beach?"

Connor leaned back in his chair. "No, but some divers do. Why are you asking these questions? Is Max in trouble?"

Patty ignored his question. "Who, other than Max, do you know who fishes at Macklyn Cove?"

Connor and Trevor glanced at each other again. Connor shrugged his shoulders.

"There's a guy we met once who fishes with Max. His name's Stuart. I don't know his last name. Other than him, maybe someone who works at the harbor knows."

Rick gave his business card to each of the guys. "Call us if you see the guy in the photo or think of something that might help us to find him."

"Sure," said Connor.

Patty and Rick left the restaurant and walked back to their car.

"What do you think?" Patty asked.

Rick smiled. "I think I'd better get back here soon when I have time for lunch."

"Yeah. Me too. And about Connor and Trevor?"

"Hard to tell the truth from the lies. You?"

Patty got into the car and looked out the window at the waves rolling in. "Why'd they have a problem with our questions? Connor hesitated with his answers a few times, especially when you were asking about fishing with Max in Brookings. But why not just tell the truth?"

Rick drove back to the highway and turned north toward Bandon. "Either they don't want to say anything that would help us, or they don't want to be associated with Max. Connor mentioned the Macklyn Cove area. I'd like to talk again with Max and his friend Stuart about the diving there."

"And let's separate them this time," said Patty.

Patty waited for Rick's response which didn't come. "You deep in thought?"

"No. Just thinking about lunch. Where do you want to eat?"

"Wherever we see the shortest line. I'm hungry too, and it's all good. We can stop in at Winter River Books after lunch."

Patty pulled her cell phone out and called Brad. "Hey, Brad. Rick and I want to talk again with Max Rainy and Stuart Trout. Can you set that up? In the interview room if they'll come in. We'll want to talk with them individually. They can come in after three-thirty today or tomorrow between nine and eleven. Also, we need you to run a Connor Brown and Trevor Hartlyn. Let us know if you find anything. Thanks."

* * *

Patty was at her desk when Brad stopped in. "I ran your guys, and both have records for petty theft. Most recent is Trevor, who stole a bike last year. You've got appointments with Max and Stuart tomorrow at nine-thirty and ten."

Patty smiled at Brad. "They agreed to come in? You must have used your charm."

Brad smiled back. "No, but I might have forgotten to give them an option."

25

Patty sat back in her chair. "I've heard memory is a tricky thing as we age."

"I must be getting up there," said Brad.

Rick walked into the office with a plate of cookies. He offered one to Patty.

"No, thanks. My stomach is still working on the lunch I ate. Where do you put it all?"

Rick looked at the plate. "It's only a few cookies. I'll wear those off just walking back and forth to the break room." Patty's laugh was one of warmth.

"We've got appointments tomorrow morning with Max Rainy and Stuart Trout. They'll come here."

"Glad they're cooperating," said Rick. "But then it doesn't surprise me. Brad's bedside manner works every time."

Rick bit into his cookie, and Patty looked up from her report. "You still miss those bacon-topped maple bars you used to eat?"

Rick furrowed his eyebrows as if contemplating how to respond. "I do. However, I understand the owner's desire to retire. It's just that no one else around here makes them, and I've not yet found a suitable replacement. There was just something about the mixture of tastes. Kind of like letting your bacon slide into your pancake's maple syrup."

"I'm sorry," said Patty. "I wish I could say that I feel your pain, but I just don't get it."

Rick smiled. "Yeah, maybe it's a guy thing. Anyway, I'm ready to call it a day. All that driving has me worn out."

"I don't remember the driving bothering you a few years ago. Must be the big five-O on the horizon."

Rick shook his head as he put on his jacket. "I've still got a few years before I reach the half-century mark. And remember, you're not that far behind me. But I guess I do find myself more frequently enjoying the ocean view and counting the years before I can walk the beach at any time of the day."

Patty put down her file and gathered her things. "That sounds nice. Let me know when you're ready to walk the beach and I'll join you."

Rick paused. "You interested in an early dinner?"

"Thanks, but I'm hoping to catch Becky for dinner before she becomes fully engrossed in her studies."

"How's she doing?"

"She seems to be doing fine. She loves living and going to school in Wyoming, and she's thinking she'd like to concentrate on larger animals. I plan to ask if she'd restrict her vet work to horses and cattle. It's great to have her home for a couple of weeks."

"Becky's a hard worker, Patty. You did good. She still dating the guy she was in love with a few years ago?"

Patty sighed. "That's something else I want to talk with her about over dinner. I'm wondering if they are growing apart."

"Long-distance relationships are hard to keep up under any circumstances," said Rick. "Well, hope you get time together."

"Thanks, Rick. See you in the morning."

Rick left the building, got into his car, and sat quietly. He started the engine and drove to the AA meeting scheduled to start in fifteen minutes. He arrived and sat at the back of the room, where he felt more comfortable.

A young woman walked in and sat two seats to his left. Rick greeted her. "Hello. I see I'm not the only one sitting where I can make a quick exit if I need to."

The woman nodded and looked back down at her hands folded in her lap. "Yes. I'm not sure I'll stay."

"First time?" asked Rick.

"Is it that evident?"

"Well, there's nothing wrong with being nervous. I was too at my first meeting. To be honest, I'm still nervous sometimes when I walk in. If it's any consolation, it gets easier."

The woman looked up at Rick. "Thanks. That's good to know."

Rick extended his hand. "My name's Rick."

The woman slowly reached out. "Stella."

When the meeting was over, Stella stood to leave and Rick quickly spoke up. "Hope to see you here again."

Stella turned to look at Rick. "You will. This was helpful." She then turned toward the door and walked out of the room.

CHAPTER FOUR

Patty arrived home before Becky and started dinner.

"Hi, Mom," Becky called as she entered the house.

"Hi, Bec. I'm in the kitchen just finishing up dinner for us."

Becky walked in and gave her mom a hug. "Smells wonderful. Anything I can do to help?" At twenty-two, Rebecca O'Toole looked like a younger version of her mother. Her green eyes gave her the nickname Cat with some of the college kids. Adding to the resemblance was her black hair that she wore shoulder-length.

"You can open that bottle of wine and pour us each a glass. I just need to cut a few slices off this roast. Everything else is on the table."

Becky poured the wine and looked at the roast. "This is a real treat for me after months of TV dinners and snack food."

Patty set the meat on the table. "Don't you ever prepare a proper meal for yourself?"

Becky laughed. "Look who's talking. The queen of TV dinners."

"Yeah, okay. You got me there. Shall we say a prayer before eating?"

Becky smiled. "Sure, Mom. Long as our dinner doesn't get cold while you run through the list of people you're praying for." She then listened to her mother's prayer and ended with an enthusiastic "Amen" before reaching for the plate of roast. "So, Mom. This is timely, us having dinner together."

"It is?"

"Yeah. I've got a couple of things to talk about."

"Well, I have a couple of questions for you too."

"Oh. Well, go ahead, Mom."

"No, you first."

Becky set her fork down. "Okay. Josh and I are breaking up."

"You've got tears in your eyes, Becky. Is this something to which you've both agreed?"

"We both agreed, Mom. It's hard, and we'll always be good friends, but we've just kind of grown apart."

Patty took a sip of wine and sat back in her chair. "How so?"

Becky looked down at her plate and moved the green beans around with her fork.

"Well, for one thing, he doesn't want to have animals in the house. Actually, he doesn't want them at all. He says he wants to have the freedom to leave for the night without having to, beforehand, plan for an animal's care during the time we'd be gone."

Patty nodded. "Well, it's good he knows what he wants and will share that with you. What about you?"

"I want to have land so that I can have lots of animals. And I'll just hire someone to care for them when I'm gone."

"Hmmm," said Patty. "You both seem pretty well set on the subject. Did you only learn this about each other recently?"

Becky put her fork down. "We hadn't previously discussed it, Mom. We were both so engrossed with our studies that the subject of pets just never came up. I don't know how to explain it, but we've just changed."

"That's very normal, Bec. Talking to each other about this shows not only the maturity you and Josh have, but also your respect and care for each other. Being apart might be good for you both. I'm pleased you both want to remain friends."

Becky smiled. "Yeah, I am too. But surely he'd have known I'd want pets since my goal was to be a vet."

"You can't expect him to have read your mind, Becky. Remember that he's been working hard on reaching his goals just as you've been working on yours. It's not fair to expect someone else to know what we want if we don't tell them."

Patty waited for Becky to respond.

"I see what you're saying, Mom. I never really told Josh I wanted a bunch of animals to live with us."

Patty smiled at her daughter. "It's good for you and Josh to explain to each other how your needs have changed. And there's nothing unusual, at your age, in making changes in what you want and need. That's what your early years are for. It will help you to make better choices later in life."

Becky looked up at her mother. "You didn't make a very good decision when you chose my dad. Do you regret marrying him?"

Patty paused before responding. "I married your dad because I was in love with him, Becky. We didn't have the wisdom you and Josh are showing by discussing, before marriage, what we each wanted out of life. Your dad left because he found someone who made him happier than he was with us. I don't understand his thinking. It's just a fact.

"But let me make something truly clear to you, Rebecca O'Toole. Through my marriage with your dad, I became a mother to a beautiful, sweet baby who has grown into a wonderful young woman and, for that reason alone, I have never regretted for one second marrying your dad. I'd do it all over again to have you in my life."

Becky smiled. "I'm sorry things between you and Dad didn't work out, Mom. But I'm glad to be here."

Patty smiled and then got up to clear the table. "Now, what was the second thing you wanted to talk about?"

"Oh, yeah, of course. The second thing is that I don't know for sure if I still want to be a vet."

Patty placed their plates in the sink and took the ice cream out of the freezer. "Well, that's a big change."

"Yeah, well, people who want to work with animals have a lot more choices today about professions. I've been studying about equine therapy and horse psychology. I can use what I've studied so far and take the necessary psychology classes. I can still work with horses and other large animals."

Patty set a dish of ice cream on the table for each of them. "And you think you'd enjoy that more than being a vet?"

"The more I read up on it, yes. I could help train horses to assist in therapy for kids. And I could have my own business and travel to meet with my patients. I think I'd enjoy being a horse psychologist."

"Well, Bec, you never cease to amaze me. Have you spoken with your school counselor about the shift in your major?"

"I have, and she figures it's doable. I'll finish school in about two years, a year earlier than I'd planned."

"Well, I want you to be happy, Becky. So I'll support you in whatever decision you make."

"Thanks, Mom." Becky ate a spoonful of ice cream. "So what were the questions you had for me?"

Patty smiled. "You've already answered them."

CHAPTER FIVE

Rick yawned as he walked into the office with a cup of coffee in one hand and a small white bakery bag in the other. "Good morning. How'd your dinner go with Becky?"

Patty looked up from the computer monitor. "It was good. Big changes are going on in her life."

"Oh, yeah?"

Patty breathed deeply then slowly exhaled. "She and Josh have broken up, and she's not sure she wants to be a vet."

Rick chuckled. "Is that all?"

"It is. The agreement to break up is mutual just because they've grown apart. And she still wants to work with animals, possibly as an equine therapist or psychologist."

"Like Dr. Doolittle or the horse whisperer?"

Patty took a doughnut out of the bag Rick brought in. "I'm not sure myself. Maybe a little of both."

Patty's desk phone rang. "It's the front office." She answered the phone and asked the receptionist to hold as she turned to Rick. "Max and Stuart are here. Who do you want to talk with first?"

"Stuart," said Rick.

Patty spoke again to the receptionist. "Ask Brad to put Stuart in the interview room and have Max wait in reception." Patty ended the call, and she and Rick walked up the hall.

Stuart sat with his back against the wall at a table that was bolted to the floor. The detectives sat across from the young man with their backs to the one-way mirror. Patty led the interview.

"Thanks for coming in, Stuart. We have just a few more questions."

"Sure. Have you found that guy you were looking for?"

"Not yet," said Patty. "We're hoping you might help us out."

Stuart shrugged and slid down in the chair. "I don't know him, so I don't know how I can help you."

"We've spoken to Connor and Trevor, and they've spent time fishing with you and Max. Surely you remember fishing with them."

Stuart shrugged again.

Rick leaned forward as Patty took a more relaxed position in her chair.

"Is that a yes?" Rick asked.

"Yeah. I guess we fished with them."

"How many times?"

Stuart hesitated like he didn't know what to say.

Patty interrupted the silence. "You seem to have a hard time talking without Max at your side. Is there some reason why you don't think you can talk to us about Connor and Trevor?"

Stuart fidgeted in the chair. "No. I just don't remember too well. We could have fished with them more than once. I can't really remember."

Rick made notes while Patty continued.

"When you and Max did fish with Connor and Trevor, where in Brookings did you go?"

Stuart looked at the ceiling as he answered. "Well, you'll have to ask Max."

"We will ask Max. But right now I'm asking you. Did you fish out at the port?"

"Could have been. We fish there a lot."

"What about Macklyn Cove?"

Stuart fidgeted in his seat. "It's been a long time since Max and I were there. I don't remember anyone else fishing there with us."

"Okay," said Patty. "You know, Stuart, if we find something's happened to Jerry, and you know where he is and are not telling us, you're going to face prison time for being an accessory to the crime even if you weren't directly involved."

Stuart sank back in his chair again. Patty looked at Rick, who put his pen and pad on the table before speaking.

"Do you understand, Stuart? It's important that you understand because we don't believe you're telling us the truth So do you understand that you will face prison time if you know something about Jerry's whereabouts and are not telling us?"

"Yeah. I've told you all I know."

Patty looked at Rick. He stood up and walked to the door. Brad had been observing the interview through the one-way window and saw that the detectives were done. He walked into the hall knowing that Rick would step out of the interview room to give him instructions about what to do next.

"We're not going to get anything useful from him," said Rick. "Return him to reception and bring Max back with you."

Brad nodded. Rick opened the door for Stuart. "Officer Bradley will take you back to reception."

Rick took his seat at the table. "Well, that was pretty futile. Let's hope Max does a little more talking."

Patty nodded. "We can conclude after this that Max is the decision-maker. Stuart probably does no independent thinking. It's like Darci Lynne and her puppets." Patty paused and looked at Rick, who was clearly not following.

"Darci who?"

Patty smiled. "She's a young ventriloquist who's become famous over the past several years. Max is like the ventriloquist and Stuart's the dummy."

"Oh. Good analogy."

The door opened, and Brad sent Max in to be interviewed.

Patty pointed at the chair. "Please sit down."

Max walked to the table and recklessly plopped down onto the chair, making the legs of the chair screech. "I don't know what else I can tell you, Detectives, but I'm happy to answer your questions if it will help you find your missing person."

"That's appreciated, Max," said Patty. "We won't keep you long."

Max looked around the room and then down at his hands that were folded on top of the table. "No problem."

Patty leaned forward in her chair to mimic Max. "We spoke with Trevor and Connor. When's the last time you fished with them?"

Max shook his head. "Oh, I don't know. Maybe two months ago. Didn't I already answer that question?"

Patty ignored the question. "Where did you fish?"

"We fish all over."

"Could you have been in Brookings?"

Max looked up and to the right, a sign considered by some to indicate lying. "Yeah, it could have been Brookings."

"Did you take your boat?"

Max exhaled loudly. "You know, we might have. But it can be foggy at this time of year, so we might have decided to fish off the jetty."

"What about Zwag Island at Macklyn Cove?" asked Patty. "Have you dived there with Connor and Trevor?"

Max flinched and fidgeted in his chair.

Patty glanced at Rick, who noted Max's reaction.

"I haven't been out there in a while. I don't think we were there with those other guys, but then Stu and I dive a lot. Sometimes other guys will see us and hang out with us just to shoot the breeze."

Patty leaned back in her chair and Rick leaned forward, picking up the questioning. "But you've fished there? At Macklyn Cove?"

"Yeah," said Max. "Mostly spearfishing."

Rick repeated his earlier question. "At Zwag Island?"

Max fidgeted again in his chair. "Yeah."

"What about Diver Rock?"

Max was quiet.

Rick paused before continuing. "Is there a reason you're not answering the question?"

"No. We've dived there too. Like I said, we've dived just about everywhere along this southern coast."

Rick leaned back and crossed his arms. "You didn't seem to want to tell us that. Why?"

Max quickly responded. "I was just trying to remember the last time we were out there. But I've answered your question. Yes, we've dived all around Macklyn Cove. So, do you dive?"

Rick leaned forward again. "Which location do you prefer? Zwag Island or Diver Rock?"

Max cleared his throat and looked up and to the right. "I guess I probably prefer Zwag Island. Now, do you have very many more questions? I promised my mom I'd run a couple errands for her. She needs her nicotine. You know how that is for smokers."

Patty looked at Rick and nodded before she turned her attention to Max. "That's all we have right now, but we may have more questions later. I think we'll take a boat ride out to Diver Rock."

Max suddenly looked a little peaked, and his eyes briefly widened. Then he stood up and walked toward the door.

"Wait there," Rick said. "I'll have Officer Bradley walk you back to reception."

After Max left, Rick and Patty returned to their office.

"What do you think?" Patty asked.

"I think we need to look closely at the Macklyn Cove area."

"I'll call the Sheriff," said Patty. "Let him know the situation and ask if he has a Search and Rescue diver who can take a look. The mention of Macklyn Cove definitely hit a nerve for Max."

Rick picked up his empty coffee cup. "I agree. Are you sure it's the county's jurisdiction and not Brookings PD or the Coast Guard?"

Patty nodded. "I am. The Sheriff has jurisdiction in the ocean within two miles of the beach."

"I didn't know that, Detective O'Toole. Thanks. Now I need a cup of coffee. Want one?'

Patty picked up her cell phone. "No, thanks."

A couple minutes later, Rick returned with his coffee and two cupcakes. He set the chocolate one on Patty's desk. She looked at the creamy-frosted cake and then looked up at Rick. "Someone's birthday?"

"Possibly, though there are no candles. Could be that nice volunteer who brings us cookies is now into cupcakes too. Getting back to the missing diver, have you heard anymore from Randy Stengle?"

"No. He just calls now and then to ask if we're any closer to finding his brother."

CHAPTER SIX

Rick bit into his cupcake. "I got a call last night from my aunt. She's coming to Brookings for a visit."

Patty put her cake down. "Your aunt? I didn't know you have an aunt. Is she on your mother or father's side of the family?"

"She's a stepsister to my dad. Her mom was my grandfather's first wife. A wife who was much younger than him. I didn't know her growing up because, after their divorce, her mom did everything she could to keep her daughter from seeing her relatives on my dad's side of the family, including my dad. After her mom remarried, they moved to Maine."

Patty scrunched her eyebrows. "That's so sad when an angry parent keeps his or her children from the other loving parent or grandparents. It seems like the cruel parent becomes so intent upon taking their anger out on another adult that they don't care if the child is hurt in the process. It happens a lot with divorced parents, and with grandparent relationships. What's your aunt's name?"

"Her name's Mary Lee, and she's to arrive late next week."

"Will she stay with you?"

"I told her she could, but she's going to stay at one of the local hotels."

"That will probably make things easier on you both since you don't know each other very well."

Rick nodded. "Definitely."

Patty turned a page in the file she was working on. "Let me know if there's anything I can do to help."

"Thanks for asking. There is. Could you join us for dinner when she gets here? I'm really at a loss as to what to talk about with her."

Patty smiled. "Sure. When you know the date and approximate time of her arrival, let me know. You can both come to dinner at my place. I'll enjoy meeting Mary Lee. Becky will too if she's home."

"Thanks. That would be great!"

Patty's phone rang and she could see that it was dispatch. "O'Toole."

"Detective O'Toole, this is Marty. We just received a call about a body in the water off Mill Beach near Diver Rock."

Patty glanced at Rick while questioning Marty. "Did you call the Sheriff?"

"I have and he's calling his SAR coordinator. If he can't come up with two local divers, he'll call Search and Rescue with other agencies."

"Who called it in?"

"The call came from a Sally Sanger. She was diving with a couple of friends. Brad and Pete are keeping them at Mill Beach for questioning."

"Okay. Rick and I are leaving now."

Rick had already put his jacket on in preparation for leaving. Patty put her phone back into her pocket and grabbed her jacket off the back of the chair.

"A body's been found near Diver Rock. It's in full diving gear, including a tank. The Sheriff's been notified and he's calling SAR."

The detectives left their office and walked to Rick's car. He drove while Patty hit speed-dial for the Sheriff.

He answered on the second ring. "Detective O'Toole. I've notified my lead SAR coordinator. Two divers will be there within the hour. I've also got Detective Finley on his way."

"Thanks, Sheriff. I wanted to let you know of our interest in the deceased. We've got a missing person who, according to his brother, was last seen before taking a diving trip with a couple of local guys. Rick and I think this could be our missing guy."

"Who are the locals your missing person is supposed to have gone diving with?"

"Max Rainy and Stuart Trout. You know the names?"

"The Rainy name sounds familiar. Could be from a while back. If there's a body, my guys will find it and drop it off at Redwood Memorial for Doc Miller. I'll ask the doc to keep you in the loop regarding identification and cause of death. I suggest our agencies work together on this."

"Thanks, Sheriff. We'd appreciate that."

Rick parked near the entrance to the cove and looked at Patty. "There's a good chance this is our missing guy."

Patty nodded. "Yes, and Max Rainy and Stuart Trout may have just become our prime suspects."

Patty and Rick parked on the street and walked down the entrance path to Mill Beach.

Brad and Pete were on the beach talking with three women in dive suits. All three women looked distressed, one more than the others. Brad saw the detectives and stepped away from the women.

"Hey, Brad," said Patty. "These the women who found our dead diver?"

Brad looked toward the women and back to Patty. "They were diving together. The one who found him is the woman crying. Her name is Mary. She's pretty shook up."

"Understandable," said Patty. "We'll talk with them separately, starting with Mary. You and Pete can ask the other two to sit down while they wait. Keep them separated."

Patty and Rick approached the women and Patty spoke to Mary. "We're Detectives O'Toole and Starker. We understand you're the one who discovered the body."

Mary nodded as tears continued to flow from her swollen eyes, red from crying. She attempted to suppress a sob, which resulted in several whimpers. One of the officers had provided her with tissues.

Patty continued. "I'm sure that must have been quite a shock. Can you tell us how it happened?"

Mary blew her nose. "Well, my friends and I have been planning this trip for two months. They are nurses, one at each of our local hospitals, and I'm a dental assistant. It's tough trying to coordinate our schedules. Sally knew we could enter the water from the beach, so we decided to dive here.

"The conditions today were perfect. No wind or fog. Well, we all swam out to Diver Rock. Sally and Tammy stopped to look at a group of abalone while I swam ahead of them. I came upon a forest of seaweed and thought I saw something silver. The seaweed was slowly swaying back and forth with the movement of the water. And then I saw…" Mary stopped to catch her breath. She stood with her hands tightly clenched, one around the used tissue.

"It was like a nightmare. I saw his arm rise in the water and slowly wave as if beckoning me to come closer. I swam forward just enough to see the silver again and realized it was his air tank. He was dead. It was horrible!"

Patty glanced at Rick and then back to Mary. "I'm sure it was. Did your friends also see the body?"

"Oh, yes. I swam back to them and pointed. They followed me and saw the man when I pointed toward his tank. Sally got Tammy's and my attention and pointed up, meaning we should all surface. We swam back to shore, and Sally called 911."

Patty placed her hand on Mary's shoulder. "Okay, Mary. Thank you. You can go sit down now while we talk with your friends."

Patty asked Sally to step away from her friends so that she could answer a few questions.

Sally's answers were similar to those of Mary. Patty thanked her and directed her to sit down again. Sally started to walk away and then turned around, facing the detectives. "Poor guy. He must have somehow panicked, thinking he was caught up in the seaweed."

"Why do you say that?" Patty asked. "You don't think he could have got himself tangled up in the stuff?"

Sally shook her head. "Well, that's what's curious. The water depth next to the rock is only about twenty-five feet. If he did get himself caught up in sea-weed, why didn't he just slip out of his vest and swim to the surface? It doesn't make sense that he'd simply lie there with his vest on."

Patty glanced at Rick as he responded to Sally. "Would slipping out of his vest have been easy for him?"

"It would if he knew he was in trouble."

"Thank you, Sally," Patty said. "Officer Bradley or Officer Chekowski will take your contact information in the event we need to get ahold of you again."

"They already have," said Sally. "Is there any way for me to find out how the man died? Can I call you?"

"We can't give you that information during our investigation, but you can call us in a few weeks."

Rick pulled a business card from his pocket and gave it to Sally.

Sally looked at the card and then up at Rick. "Thank you, Detective Starker. I'll call."

The detectives interviewed the third diver and then left the three women with Brad and Pete. A Coast Guard boat was sitting offshore to provide back up to the Sheriff.

When they looked back at the park entrance, they could see that it was getting crowded with representatives from several law enforcement agencies. Detective Michelle Finley from the Sheriff's Office stepped out of the crowd and approached Patty and Rick.

Patty smiled. "Detective Finley, good to see you."

The petite woman smiled. "And you as well, Detective O'Toole." She then turned her attention toward Rick. "Decided to come home to where the real work gets done, eh, Detective Starker?"

Rick laughed. "You've got me figured out, Finley. It's good to be back."

"We've spoken," Patty said, "with the three women who found the body. We'll type up our notes and share the information. You might want to check in with Brad and Pete."

Detective Finley walked over to where Brad was waiting for the SAR diver.

Patty looked out at the gentle waves lapping at the shore. "So why did the diver drown? Was he dead before he hit the water? Did someone hold him down until he drowned? If something had ripped his hose, he could still have swum to the top."

"Or," said Rick, "did someone incapacitate him before throwing him overboard?"

"You mean was he drugged?"

"That's what I'm thinking," said Rick. "Doc Miller can tell us whether or not he was dead before hitting the water, and whether he had drugs in his system."

Two divers arrived, and the detectives walked over to the beach entrance to greet them.

"I'm Detective O'Toole and this is Detective Starker. Thanks for coming."

"No problem, Detectives. I'm Blake Whitely with Curry County Search and Rescue. The Sheriff sent us. I understand a body was discovered in the water near Diver Rock."

"That's right," said Patty. "The guy is lying on the bottom. He's in a wet suit and is wearing a diving vest."

The SAR divers entered the water and swam out to where the body was found. Blake later reported that the necessary photos were taken before moving the body and bringing it up to the top where a Sheriff's boat had arrived. Three SAR members helped take the body from the divers and lift it into the boat. The divers climbed in and traveled with the body to the Port of Brookings Harbor.

Patty and Rick walked back to their car and returned to the office to begin writing up their report.

Patty's cell phone rang as she sat down at her desk. Caller ID identified her mother.

"Detective O'Toole," she said.

"I love it when you answer that way, Patty."

Patty laughed. "I know you do, Mom, and I'm glad to provide a bit of humor to your day."

"It's pride, dear daughter. So, how's your morning going? You and Rick solve any murders?"

"We've not solved any, but we may have one on our hands."

"Really? Who was murdered? Anyone I know? How? When? Do you have a suspect?"

"Slow down, Mom. I can tell you only that we've retrieved a body in the water at Macklyn Cove. You'll read about that in the paper. There's nothing else I can say about it right now."

"Okay. That sounds sad. Not what I was expecting."

"I know, Mom. Tell me how your day's going."

"Well, I have a new friend. Her name's Grace, and I met her at the senior center. We met for coffee this morning."

"Wonderful, Mom. I'm happy for you. I've got a few minutes. Tell me about her."

"Well, let's see. We only just met, so I don't know a lot. But she's seventy-five years old and moved to Brookings about four months ago. She's a widow and lives alone. She's funny and makes me laugh, though based upon something she said, I think she's had a difficult life."

"She seems like a nice person to have as a friend, Mom. What did she say that suggested to you she'd had a difficult life?"

"Oh, I guess it wasn't so much what she said but rather the sad look in her eyes when she said it. She spoke of being a single mom. She didn't go into specifics, but she got that faraway look in her eyes like she was remembering some of it. So I asked if she'd like us to change the subject and she said yes. Then I told her about the various places in Curry County that are fun or interesting to visit. We're planning to have lunch together one day next week and then visit the galleries and a few gift shops."

"That sounds fun, Mom. It will be good for you to have a friend who appreciates art the way you do."

"Yes, I'm looking forward to Grace and I getting to enjoy our time together. Well, I've got chores and I know you need to get back to work. I'm sorry, dear, about the case. I know this will be another difficult one for you."

"Thanks, Mom. Hope you enjoy your day. Love you."

"I love you too, Patty."

Patty ended the call and looked up at Rick. "This case reminds me of an incident several years ago in which we almost suffered a mass tragedy in the ocean. It would have been, had it not been for the work of our SAR volunteers."

Rick nodded. "That was before my time, though I've heard about a situation where a deputy went into the water after a boy who had been pulled out to sea, and the deputy himself got into trouble. If that's the rescue you're thinking of, I'd be interested in learning the whole story."

Patty got up and walked to the door. She could see that Brad and Pete had returned from Mill Beach. "Hey, Brad. Got a minute?"

Brad walked up to Patty. "What's up?"

"Rick wants to know about the incident several years ago when one of our deputies and a couple of SAR guys saved the boy that had been taken out to sea by an undertow and a strong current. You were with SAR. Do you know about that incident?"

Brad walked into the detective's office and sat down. "Sure, but it will have to be the abridged version. I've got a dental appointment in a few minutes. I was only a SAR member for three years, and that was long before I came to Brookings PD. But I've heard the story many times.

"A teenage boy playing in the shallow water at Harris Beach was hit by a sneaker wave and then pulled out into the ocean by an undertow. He quickly realized that he couldn't swim back to shore. A 911 call was made, and one of the responders, a young deputy, swam out to save the kid. The rescue deputy did reach the boy, but the same current that took the boy out prevented them both from swimming back to shore."

Patty sipped her coffee while Brad continued. "Their situation got a lot worse, and lives would have been lost had it not been for the quick thinking and bravery of our SAR members. I've got to leave for my dental appointment, but you need to hear the whole story. What those three men did that day is remarkable. They're all heroes in my book."

Patty nodded. "It still amazes me to think of how quickly they acted, putting their own lives in danger to save the boy's life. There aren't many people who would have jumped into the frigid water and held on out there for as long as they did. We are fortunate in this county to have such courage and commitment from those whose mission is to save lives and lower the distress of the families of those gone missing."

"That's a great rescue story," said Rick. "I knew the SAR members were called out for searches now and then, but I didn't understand to what extent they'll go to save lives. While listening to you talk, I've thought of something. I have a friend who is Scoutmaster for a local troop. He's always bringing in speakers for the Scouts on subjects they appreciate. I know he'd be grateful if you spoke to his Scouts about Curry County's Search and Rescue team. Would you be up to it if I asked him to call you?"

Brad smiled. "That's a great idea, but I was only with the Search and Rescue operation for a few years. I'll get a couple of experienced guys to join me. Some of these guys have been active for fifteen years or more. Let me talk with the SAR coordinator. I'm sure he'd be interested."

Rick smiled. "Great! My friend's name is Ralph Newport. He'll want to call and confirm a date with you. I'll give him your name and phone number if you don't mind doing the coordination."

"No problem," said Brad. "Happy to help make it come together. Educating our local young people about Search and Rescue is important. We'll need some of them to replace the old guys like me."

Brad left the office, and Rick looked down at the file on his desk.

"I think I'll finish this report tomorrow. It's been a full day. You want to schedule interviews with Max and Stuart again?"

"I do," said Patty, "but I'd like to wait until we hear from Doc Miller about cause of death. I'm going to do a little more work here. See you tomorrow."

CHAPTER SEVEN

Rick left the office and walked through the parking lot to his car. He slipped inside and sat for a moment. Then he started the engine and drove to the evening AA meeting. He chose a seat in the back and looked around for Stella. She wasn't there. He looked at his watch to see that he was four minutes early. He looked again two minutes later, leaned back into the seat, exhaled, and closed his eyes.

"All right if I sit here?"

Rick opened his eyes to see Stella pointing toward the seat next to him. He sat up straight and smiled. "I've been saving that seat for you."

Before they could begin a conversation, the meeting began. An hour and a half later, it came to an end.

Stella stood up, and Rick quickly stood up next to her.

"Would you like to go get something to eat?" he asked.

"That would be nice."

They chose a local restaurant, were shown to their seats, and sat down facing each other.

Stella was the first to speak.

"In the meeting, you mentioned it's been four years. For how long did you drink?"

Rick took hold of the water glass and moved his hand around on the glass, causing condensation to drip onto the wooden table. He stared silently into Stella's eyes.

Stella looked down at the table and then back up at Rick. "I'm sorry if I've made you uncomfortable. You don't have to answer that. I just wondered because I've only been sober fifteen months, and I was going to ask a few questions about what I could expect."

Rick nodded. "It's no problem. It's just that it's been a while since I've spoken about this to anyone. I want you to ask your questions.

"I drank since I was in college, but it never got out of hand. That is, until nine years ago, when my wife and daughter were murdered. I was a detective in Boston at the time. I was not allowed to work the case. A year after their deaths, the case had not been solved and was put on the shelf with other cold cases. I knew I had to do something different from showing up at work every day and then going home to drink myself into oblivion so that I could sleep. I wanted to get as far away as I could from Boston and everything a big city represented. So I moved to Brookings. I took a job here and was in the process of rebuilding my life when the drinking got out of hand again. This time, my partner and lead detective, Patty O'Toole, helped me solve my wife and daughter's murder. The responsible was convicted of several crimes and put away for life.

"Solving that case changed something in my head, and I no longer wanted to drink. So I went to two or three meetings and found they helped. Haven't drunk since."

Stella stared into Rick's eyes. "I'm so sorry about your wife and daughter. I can't imagine such loss."

Rick nodded. "I wouldn't expect you to."

The waitress arrived with meatloaf and mashed potatoes for Rick, and fish and chips for Stella. They each took a bite of their respective dinners, and Stella put down her fork.

"I started drinking in high school to be one of the crowd. I guess you'd call it peer pressure. On Friday and Saturday evenings we'd all pitch in, someone would buy the booze, and we'd hang out at one of the local parks. In college the drinking continued. It was almost expected.

"In my second year, I met the so-called man-of-my-dreams, and we married. That's when the abuse started. He'd leave at all hours of the night and several days at a time, always with an excuse. At night he'd have to go for long walks because he couldn't sleep. He was a leasing agent for a large national franchise and would leave for days to check out new locations and negotiate leases.

"The longer we stayed together, the lower my self-esteem fell. I dropped out of school and went to work full-time at a job I didn't enjoy. Every night I'd go home and have several drinks to mask the pain. I knew something wasn't right, but I couldn't get up the nerve to leave. I just didn't think I could make it on my own.

"That went on for twelve years. Then, one day I read a book about a woman who'd experienced similar emotional abuse. In the story, she found an organization that helped abused women. So I sought one out in my area and got help. Just having someone listen to and care about me was enough to make me want to stop drinking.

"My counselor told me about AA, but I'm not a group kind of person. I filed for divorce, quit the job I had, and went to work doing something I enjoy. That was fifteen months ago, and I haven't had a drink since. I like myself a lot better than I did when I drank, and through counseling I've learned that I'm a good person and worthy of happiness. Finalization of the divorce took a while, and when it ended, my counselor suggested again that I attend an AA meeting now and then as sort of a healthy check-up." Stella picked up her water and took a sip. She looked up at Rick. "I don't know what this means to you, but our telling each other our stories feels kind of scary to me. Good, but scary."

Rick sat quietly. Stella noticed that Rick had finished his meal. She took a bite of her fish. She swallowed and put down her fork again. "What are you thinking?"

Rick took a slow deep breath. "Well, I'm thinking that I'd like to see you again. But I'm also thinking that our seeing each other would involve risk, and risk can result in pain. And we both took to drinking to mask our pain."

"I understand the concern. I guess I figure life is full of pain. We've each figured out that drinking doesn't take away the cause of the pain but rather simply pushes forward the time in which we must face it. I'd like to see you too. Let's both agree that we'll move forward slowly, with kindness and understanding toward each other. And if either of us wants a time-out, no problem."

"Agreed," said Rick. "Do you like to walk on the beach or hike?"

Stella smiled. "Yes."

"What about Sunday? I could pick you up and we'll go to Harris Beach State Park. If we walk the beach and want to do some additional hiking, we'll go north."

Stella pulled a pen and small pad out of her purse and wrote something down. She handed it to Rick. "My address and phone number."

Rick gave Stella one of his cards. "If for any reason you can't make it or you change your mind, give me a call." He looked at Stella's plate. "If you want to finish your dinner and not eat alone, I could order a piece of pie."

"Oh, sure. I'm kind of a slow eater. But I would like to finish it."

Rick flagged the waiter, then asked Stella, "Would you like pie too? Maybe take it home to go with your coffee in the morning?"

"I'd like that. You're a very thoughtful guy."

Rick sort of half-smiled. "You wouldn't be teasing me, would you?"

Stella laughed. "No. Why would you think that?"

"Because I'm really hungry for a piece of pie."

Stella looked Rick in the eyes. "And you think that I know that your offer to keep me from eating alone was just to get your end result—a piece of pie."

There was silence between them, and then they both broke out in grins.

"You've got me there," he said.

CHAPTER EIGHT

The following Monday, Patty and Rick were at their desks early. Patty's cell phone rang.

"It's the doc." Rick put down his pen and picked up his coffee cup.

"Hi, Doc. Rick and I are in the office with you on speaker phone. How was your weekend?"

"Weekend? Oh, is that what that was? I was in here all day Saturday. But then, I can't complain. I remember while still in school, my anatomy instructor promising all of us students that, should we become medical examiners or coroners, we'd never have to worry about unemployment. We figured he meant that we'd have a forty-hour a week job with benefits and five weeks of vacation a year. Huh!! Little did we know."

"I guess," said Patty, "that none of us really knew what all the job entailed when we signed up."

Doc Miller laughed. "You do know, don't you?"

"We do. So, what have you got for us, Doc? Figured out what killed our diver?"

"This is a curious one, Patty. I know how his death was initiated, and I know how he was incapacitated, but I don't yet have the solution that must have been injected."

"Can you begin with how the death was initiated?"

"Someone smeared peanut oil over Jerry's mouthpiece. Whoever did it knew he was allergic to peanuts and that the slight bit of oil could cause anaphylaxis."

"That alone could kill someone, Doc. Why do you think that only initiated his death?"

"Because I found a small injection between his fingers. I could have easily missed it if I hadn't become suspicious after learning about the peanut oil. Your killer may not have known to what degree the small amount of peanut oil would incapacitate your victim and wanted to make sure he died in the water. So he injected your victim with a drug we've not yet identified."

Patty glanced up at Rick. "That certainly leaves no question about premeditation. Any idea, Doc, on how you think the killer got the victim into the ocean and injected him with no other divers noticing?"

"That's a question for you and Rick to solve, Patty. I can tell you what substances killed him, but you two will figure out the circumstances around his death."

"Well, thanks, Doc. Does the Sheriff know?"

"Yes. I called him first since the body was found in his jurisdiction. You have any suspects?"

"No. A couple persons of interest but no suspects."

"Yet," said the doc.

"Right," said Rick. "We'll find the responsible."

"I know you will," said the doc. "You two be careful out there."

"Thanks, Doc," said Patty.

Patty ended the call, and she and Rick sat quietly for a minute. "Let's talk to Jerry's brother again. Confirm whether Jerry had a peanut allergy and, if he did, who might have known."

Rick picked up the phone. "I'll call him now. You have time if we're able to see him this afternoon?"

"I do, and the sooner the better."

Rick called and was able to talk with Randy Stengle. "To confirm, we'll be at your home at one o'clock."

Patty looked at her calendar. "I'll ask Brad to bring Max and Stuart back in here tomorrow. Does it matter to you if it's morning or afternoon?"

Rick's phone rang. "No," he responded to Patty and then answered the phone. "Detective Starker."

"Hi, Detective. This is Mike Olford down at the harbor."

"Hi, Mike. What's up?"

"Well, I heard about the body being found over at Macklyn Cove and just wanted you to know that three guys from Oakland, CA were here a few days before your body was found."

Rick picked up his pencil. "Yeah? What about them?"

"Well, the first day after arriving, they left here in the early morning. Said they were going out for rockfish. That afternoon I bumped into two of them on the dock. I asked about their catch and where the third guy was."

"What was their response?"

"They said that he got seasick and was below deck sleeping."

Rick put his pencil down. "And you didn't believe them?"

"Well, it's just that I see most of what goes on down there, and I saw the third guy on the dock an hour later. The next day, their boat was gone. I assumed they went back to Oakland. I just thought you'd want to know."

"Okay, that's good, Mike. Give me their names and contact information, and we'll check it out."

Mike gave two names and numbers to Rick. "I never got information from the third guy."

"Would you recognize the guy if you saw a picture of him?"

"No. I only saw him from the back when he was walking down the plank. I was busy processing their moorage fee at that time."

"Thanks, Mike."

"Sure, Detective."

Rick gave Patty the information. "I'll get ahold of these guys and find out why they were in Brookings."

"We can run the two names you have by Randy, too," said Patty. "Find out if they're familiar to him. We'll need to give ourselves a couple hours to get there. Work is still ongoing on 199 due to last year's fires, so it's slow. We should leave after you make your calls to the two boaters."

Rick called both boaters and then prepared to leave with Patty. "They are up at the Gold Beach harbor right now but will be in our office tomorrow morning at ten."

"They must be traveling up the coast fishing. Did the guy you spoke with suggest that we were interrupting their plans to go north to Port Orford?"

"He didn't say. Just said they'd be here at ten."

Patty picked up her jacket. "Let's go talk to Randy Stengle. You can drive."

Rick smiled. "No problem."

On the way to Cave Junction Rick commented on the accident statistics for 199. "Do you know this is one of the deadliest highways in the nation?"

"I do. There are plenty of signs telling people to slow down. A lot of travelers aren't used to the hairpin curves we have on this highway. If you don't make the turn, your choice is to drive into a wall of rock, drive over the side of the canyon, or hit another driver. The beautiful sights of the river and surrounding forest can take one's eyes off the road at the wrong moment. I'm sure a lot of lives have been shattered due to accidents. Lives of those involved and their families."

Rick drove in silence for most of the trip before Patty spoke again.

"Brad told me that the SAR talk to the Scouts will be this Thursday at six P.M. I'm going to attend. Want to join me to support our local heroes?"

"Yeah, I do. I'm interested in learning more about some of their calls that resulted in searches."

The detectives pulled into the driveway of Randy Stengle's home. Rick turned off the engine and paused. "So if what Stengle said is true, this house was left to him and his brother when their parents died. According to him, the brothers got along great. But what if he's lying?"

Patty unhooked her seat belt. "You mean what if Randy got rid of his brother to fully own the house?"

Rick nodded.

"It's a possibility," said Patty, "which leads to the question of whether he really doesn't know Max Rainy."

Rick looked at Patty. "They could be in this together."

Patty nodded. "Let's go talk with him."

Randy opened the door as the detectives walked up the five steps to the front porch.

"Good afternoon," said Patty.

"Hi, Detectives. Come on in."

Patty and Rick followed him to a small living room area, where they all sat down.

Randy lit up a cigarette. "Are you any closer to finding my brother?"

Patty spoke softly. "We've found the body of a diver, Randy, but we've not yet identified him. The deceased does have a unique tattoo. Can you tell me if Jerry has any tattoos?"

Randy took a drag from his cigarette and slowly blew the smoke out. "Just one, on his back. It's an old diver's helmet. You know, like what was used in the movie *Twenty Thousand Leagues Under The Sea*?"

Patty glanced at Rick and then turned back to Randy. "That is the tattoo described to us by the medical examiner. We'll continue with the DNA testing, but we now believe the deceased is Jerry."

Randy stood up and walked to the window where he could look out at the lush forest surrounding his house.

"I was afraid this is how it would turn out. He's just been gone for too long without checking in with me." He turned back around to face the detectives. "Do you know how he died?"

"The medical examiner is still working on it, but we believe your brother was murdered."

"Why would anyone want to murder Jerry?"

Rick stood up. "That's what we need to find out. Do you know if Jerry had an allergy?"

Randy nodded. "He was allergic to peanuts. Why do you ask?"

"Because there was a trace of peanut oil on his mouthpiece."

"Peanut oil? That would have killed him, at least without immediate medical care."

"Who else would have known about Jerry's peanut allergy?"

Randy thought for a moment. "I don't know. We never really talked about it. He just knew to be careful."

"We've got a few more names we want to run by you," said Rick, "and a couple of photos we want you to look at." Rick read off the names of the two boaters who were going to be interviewed the next day.

"I've never heard of them," said Randy.

"What about Trevor Hartlyn or Connor Brown?"

"No."

"And you're sure you haven't met Max Rainy or Stuart Trout?"

"I only know Max's name because of the high school connection with Jerry and his fishing trip when he left here. I don't know any of those other names."

Rick showed him photos of Trevor, Connor, Max, and Stuart.

Randy took the photos and looked through them one at a time. "I recognize Max but not the others."

Patty stood up. "Do you know if you're Jerry's beneficiary for his half of this house?"

Randy looked across the room at Patty. "Beneficiary? I don't know. I don't think Jerry had a will or trust. But I hope I get his half because I don't want to move."

Patty stepped up to Randy and took the photos from his hands. "Do you dive?"

Randy shook his head. "No. Never. I'm afraid to put my head under the water."

Rick pointed toward a hallway. "Is Jerry's room down here?"

Randy turned his head toward the hallway. "Yeah."

"Mind if we look at his room? We might find something that will help lead us to his killer."

"Sure," said Randy. "It's the first room on the left."

Patty and Rick walked down the hall and opened the door to Jerry's room. The blinds were drawn, creating an eerie darkness on an otherwise sunlit day. Rick turned on the overhead light.

Looking around the room, Rick picked up a picture frame on the dresser and showed the photo to Randy. "That was quite a catch. Is this Jerry?"

"Yeah. That was taken about four years ago. Jerry caught that fishing off the jetty at the mouth of the Chetco. He was pretty excited."

"Were you there with him?"

"I was."

"Who else was there?"

"I don't know. Just a couple of guys that know Jerry. They were fishing too."

"Do you remember their names?"

"No. It was too long ago. Jerry fished a lot and was always talking with other guys about their catch. I didn't pay much attention to who the guys were."

Patty took the photo from Rick. "This could be important, Randy. Do you remember any part of the conversation?"

"Well, I guess the other guys mentioned fishing in Port Orford a lot. You know, I sort of remember that one of them could have been named Connor."

"Do you remember anything else that was said that may have given you the impression this wasn't a first meeting between Jerry and the other two guys?"

"Well, I think it was the first time they'd met because they didn't seem like old friends."

Patty set the photo down and looked around the room. "Your brother sure liked diving photos and gear. I'm surprised he hadn't kept up his certification."

"Yeah. I guess I am too. I haven't been in this room in a long time."

Rick moved around a few things on Jerry's desk.

"There's a calendar here with the date marked out that you last saw him. He wrote, 'Brookings dive.' He could have been planning on meeting with several divers rather than just Max."

Randy shrugged. "Could be. He just told me that he was going diving with Max."

Patty glanced at Rick, and the two of them walked out of the room. Patty stopped in the hallway and spoke to Randy. "Long as we're here, do you mind if we take a look around the house?"

Randy hesitated and looked down the hall. "Well, it's not a good time for me. I've got someplace to be in about ten minutes."

"No problem," said Patty. "We won't be long."

"Well, okay."

Three minutes later, the detectives thanked Randy and left.

"It's pretty clean," said Patty as she and Rick started back to Brookings.

"It is. The trauma of losing one's parents could have pushed a lot of teenagers over the edge. Instead, it seems to have given Randy and Jerry the strength to process their grief without drugs or heavy use of alcohol. I imagine that their having each other helped them a lot."

CHAPTER NINE

The meeting was held in the local Elks Club, which provided a raised area for the speakers. About twenty Scouts were seated in rows, with what appeared to be parents and family members seated behind them. Patty and Rick found seats at the back of the room.

The Scoutmaster started the evening off by introducing Brad, Blake, and Tod. Then Brad took the microphone.

"Hello, Scouts. My name is Burt Bradley, and I'm an officer with your Brookings Police Department. I was also a member of the organization that is the subject for your entertainment this evening, Curry County Search and Rescue. I was with Search and Rescue a long time ago, before going to work for the Brookings Police Department.

"With me this evening are two men who have each given more than fifteen years of service to Curry County's Search and Rescue program. Blake Whitely is a Search and Rescue swimmer in addition to participating in searches on land. He's going to tell you about a rescue in which he was very much involved. It happened here in Brookings about seven years ago.

"Then you'll hear from Sheriff's Sergeant Tod Hogram. Tod spends a lot of his time on the river, where he's played a primary role in many rescues and recoveries as well as searches in our surrounding forests. I'm sure you're going to have questions for our speakers, but please hold them until after you've heard from both Tod and Blake. We'll make time for questions after the talks."

Patty leaned over to Rick. "I bet Blake talks about the incident Brad told us about."

Rick nodded. "I hope so. It will be great to hear directly from one of the heroes that day."

"Before you hear from our guests, I want to set the stage for their stories. Listen carefully. This is about Curry County, the area of Oregon in which you live. The southern Oregon coast is one of the most beautiful in the world. With average annual temperatures in the high fifties and an average wind speed of sixteen miles per hour, the weather is comfortable throughout most of the year.

"But some days are not the average. Our king tide phenomenon, that occurs three times a year, can, with a heavy storm, produce twelve-to thirty-five-foot waves. Our storms can cause the wind to blow twenty-five to thirty-five miles per hour with seventy-mile-per-hour wind gusts. That's almost as high as a Category One hurricane.

"The ocean that brings great beauty to our coast can also be deadly. Sneaker waves and heavy rolling logs have taken many lives. We learn early to keep away from both of these hazards. Our giant rocks off the beach are called 'sea stacks' and can be extremely dangerous to those who decide to climb them.

"There are ten rivers in Curry County which, like the ocean, can produce a great fishing or swimming experience. But you'll learn that the rivers change over time and should always demand a healthy respect. Our forests provide great hunting and hiking opportunities, but they can also be dangerous places. Be aware of your surroundings. Learn to respect your surroundings, and you'll find great beauty and adventure here on Oregon's southern coast.

"Now I'd like to introduce Search and Rescuer Coordinator Blake Whitely."

The audience broke into applause as Blake took the stage and started right in on a rescue story.

"The day began with my receipt of a call from the Sheriff's lieutenant who oversaw the SAR program. SAR stands for 'Search and Rescue.' The lieutenant was in Gold Beach at that time. He was concerned about one of his deputies who had responded to a 911 distress call about a boy stranded in the ocean. The boy had been playing with friends along the beach when a sneaker wave knocked him over. Before the boy could get back on his feet, another wave hit, and an undertow carried him out to sea. He tried unsuccessfully to swim back toward the shore and continued to be pulled out into the ocean.

"A Sheriff's deputy was in Brookings and responded immediately to the 911 call. He ran to the beach, took off his heavy-duty belt, shoes and socks, and shirt. He put his life vest on and a backpack that will unfurl a one-hundred-foot rope. He gave the end of the rope to an officer on the beach with instructions to pull, once the deputy had hold of the boy, both himself and the boy to shore. The deputy was able to get past the waves crashing on shore. He swam toward the boy and was pulled out by the current to where the boy was treading water. He took hold of the boy and promised everything would be okay. Continuous waves washed over them as the wind picked up.

"A Coast Guard boat arrived but couldn't get close enough due to the rough sea and our rocky sea stacks. So the deputy soon found himself in trouble due to the cold water and the difficulty of holding onto the boy. He couldn't swim to shore against the strong current and the officer on the beach was unable to pull them in.

"The Sheriff's lieutenant was alerted to the situation. He knew he couldn't make the thirty-mile drive from Gold Beach to Brookings fast enough to get there and rescue his deputy and the boy. They needed help immediately. He knew that after fifteen minutes in the ocean, where the average temperature is forty to fifty degrees, hypothermia would begin to set in, and death could occur in one to three hours. He figured the boy had already been in the water more than a half hour and his deputy more than fifteen minutes.

"That's when the lieutenant called me, his Assistant Search and Rescue Coordinator. I was only about ten minutes from the beach and responded immediately to the lieutenant's request. When I got to the parking lot, I saw deputies and police and fire department officers huddled on the beach. Then I looked across the water and saw the deputy floating on his back with the boy hanging onto him. I grabbed my gear, a dry suit, helmet, and throw rope, and ran down the pathway to the beach. After several attempts, I was able to swim through the waves out to where the boy and the first rescue deputy were barely hanging on.

"The Coast Guard showed up with a bigger boat. But again they couldn't get close enough to assist due to the danger of the boat being pushed against our giant sea stacks by powerful waves. It was now about fifty minutes since the boy had first been pulled out to sea and about thirty-five minutes since the first rescue deputy had entered the water.

"I finally reached them and fought to keep their heads above water. I swam, struggling against the current, holding onto them. I got close enough to the shore to feel the sand on my back. But the strength of the undertow took us back out to sea. Now the three of us were stranded, and the cold was taking its toll.

"I remember a thought crossing my mind that it seemed as though no one was going to be able to save us. Then I looked up and saw someone in a dry suit scrambling over the rocks.

"The Sheriff's lieutenant had arrived. I knew then that we were going to be all right. He brought a three-hundred-fifty-foot rope and gave one end of it to the men on the beach. He climbed over the rocks, keeping the rope from becoming snagged, and climbed up to a short distance from the three of us in the water. He jumped into the water and began swimming through the waves. He got to within ten feet of us when he ran out of rope. At that point, I had the first rescue deputy lie on his back. I used him to bridge the distance between us and the lieutenant. The deputy, on his back, put his hands up over his head. The lieutenant was able to grab the deputy's fingers and then his hands, pulling him in with the boy and me. The lieutenant drew the three of us to him and tied the rope around us and himself. He then gave the signal to the first responders on shore to pull. We all made it!

"And that's how we rescued a young fourteen-year-old boy who went to the beach one day to play along the shore. There's a phrase you've all probably heard and need to take seriously out here: *Don't turn your back on the ocean!*"

The audience broke into loud applause and stood up in honor of Blake. When the Scouts stopped clapping, several hands went up. Brad stepped up to the mic.

"We appreciate you have questions, but we'll hold off on answering them until after you hear more about Curry County's Search and Rescue from Sergeant Hogram."

Tod stepped up to the mic. "Hi, I'm Tod Hogram. I'm a sergeant with your Curry County Sheriff's Office. I'm also a coordinator for Search and Rescue. I'm a marine deputy, therefore a lot of my time is spent on the our rivers and the ocean, where I've been involved in many rescues and recoveries. I've also participated in many rescues in our local forests.

"One rescue involved an elderly man who lived with some of his family members. The man had dementia, a disease of the mind that causes the sick person to forget who and where they are. One night the man walked away from his house and was missing for four days before one of our volunteers found him. He had walked a long way through very thick brush and thorny bushes. We were all grateful to find him alive. He spent a few days in the hospital and was then returned to his family. This was the kind of ending we hope for on all our rescues. One where we return a person who is lost or in distress back to their family. I hope that after listening to Blake and me talk about Search and Rescue, some of you may want to join us when you become of age. Thank you."

The audience was on their feet again with loud applause as Tod walked to the side of the stage. Brad and Blake joined Tod, and Brad stepped up to the mic.

"Okay, as promised, we'll now answer your questions." Brad pointed to a Scout in the front row. "What's your question, young man?"

The boy looked to be about fifteen. He respectfully stood up and asked his question. "How many calls does Search and Rescue get every year?"

Brad passed the microphone to Tod.

"On average, we get about sixty calls a year."

"Wow!" said several of the boys.

Tod continued. "Most of those result in the missing person returning home or being found very quickly, and those calls don't require a Search and Rescue team of volunteers to respond."

Brad pointed to another Scout who stood. "Does a person interested in being a member of Search and Rescue have to go through any training?"

Blake stepped up to the mic. "They do. There's a seventy-five-question written test and a First Aid class and test. The volunteer must be healthy, and he or she must spend a night in the forest. That means building a fire and a shelter, and remaining calm even if the temperature is in the low thirties."

Patty looked at Rick. "I'm learning right along with the Scouts. There's a lot more than I realized to being a member of the Sheriff's SAR program."

Brad pointed to another Scout. The young man eagerly stood to ask his question. "What should people do if they get lost in the woods? My friend told me that if I get lost, I should walk downhill if I think a river is close. Is that right?"

Brad gave Tod the mic.

"Well, your friend is misinformed. The best thing you can do is to stay with your vehicle. It's a lot easier for you to be seen by an aircraft if you're with your vehicle than if you're in the trees and brush."

The air was buzzing with Scouts whispering to each other about all that they'd learned. The Scoutmaster stepped onto the stage. "Let's have one more question before we give a final thanks to our guests. What's your question, Marvin?"

"Why do so many accidents happen on our rivers and the ocean?"

Blake glanced at Tod who took the mic. "The rivers provide a great source of recreation, but they can also be dangerous. There are rapids, eddies, and undertows. Before going out you should research the conditions and be prepared." Tod looked at Blake. "Do you have anything to add?"

"I'll repeat what Officer Bradley said earlier. Don't turn your back on the ocean. Sneaker waves are real, and water is much stronger than you can imagine."

The Scoutmaster addressed the audience. "Let's give another round of applause for our guests today."

The Scouts clapped, and the Scoutmaster turned toward Tod, Blake, and Brad. "Our troop has hiked and camped many times in these forests, and the boys have learned survival skills. Your talk here today will add to their knowledge and help with their survival if any of them should become lost. Thank you."

When Tod and Blake left the stage, Patty approached and asked if they had time for lunch. The five of them drove to a local restaurant where the conversation about Search and Rescue continued.

"That was powerful," Patty said. "I wouldn't be surprised if your talk produces at least two new SAR members over the next few years."

"It was a great education for the Scouts and me," Rick said. "I've a question for Tod that I didn't want to bring up with the kids. It has to do with drownings in the river. Why is it that some bodies rise to the surface faster than others?"

"It has to do with water temperature and the flow of the water. The warmer the water, the faster bloating will occur, and the faster the body will rise to the surface. The water flow enters the equation as well. Those of us who've been doing this for years can pretty much guess how long it will take."

CHAPTER TEN

The detectives were in their office early the next day. Rick reached into the bakery bag on Patty's desk. "Thanks for bringing breakfast."

"You're welcome. You know that I blame you for turning me into a pastry junkie."

Rick laughed. "My intent was to introduce you to one of my favorite food groups."

"Well, I'm glad you did. I would have felt that I'd missed out in life if I'd never tasted good pastry. On another note, wasn't that a great program the guys put on last night?"

"It was. I couldn't help but think, as I was watching, that the junior high and high school-aged kids should hear the talk we heard and learn about SAR. Great timing would be just before the kids get out of school for the summer, when several of them throw caution to the wind."

"That's a good idea, Rick. You might suggest it to Sergeant Hogram."

Patty's phone rang, and Brad let her know that there were three men waiting to see her and Rick.

"Three?"

"Three," said Brad. "How about I take one of them back to the interview room?"

Patty and Rick entered the room and sat down across from Terry Hall.

"Mr. Hall," greeted Patty. "I'm Detective O'Toole and this is Detective Starker. Thanks for coming in. We understand that you were in Gold Beach yesterday."

Hall looked at Patty and then Rick. "We were in Gold Beach and planned to head back home today. So it's no bother to stop here. What can I do for you?"

Rick took notes while Patty asked the questions. "Do you own a boat called *Aquarius*?"

"I'm one of the owners."

"Who owns it with you?"

"My buddy, Arnold."

"Is Arnold one of the two guys waiting in our reception room?"

"Yes."

"Where are you and your friends from?"

"Arnold and I are from Oakland, California. Our buddy lives in southern California."

"Oakland," Patty repeated. "Former home of Jack London."

Terry smiled. "I'm surprised you know that."

Rick lowered his pen. "She reads a lot."

Patty continued with her questioning. "What brought you to Brookings?"

"Nothing specific. We just wanted to check out the small towns along Oregon's coast."

"Was this your first trip to our port?"

"It was."

"How long will you stay?"

Terry squirmed a bit in his seat. "We're just here to see you and replenish our supplies. We'll take off in the morning. When your officer asked us to come in, he said that you have questions about the death of a diver you found. Is there some other reason you've brought us in?"

"Did you stop in Eureka on your way up the coast?"

"Eureka? No."

Patty glanced at Rick and then turned attention again to Terry. "Well, that's odd. I have a detective friend in Eureka who says you were docked there for two days before moving on to Brookings."

Terry slowly inhaled through his nose, held his breath, and then loudly exhaled through his mouth. For the first time during the interview he looked like he'd been caught off guard.

"Let me think. Yeah, I guess we did make a brief stop in Eureka. You know, after a while all small ports begin to look the same. We do so much traveling that I sometimes forget where I've been. Especially when we travel at night."

Patty sat back in her chair. "We have a diver who may have died the day you were here. It was probably someone in a boat who killed him. Tell us about your day in the port. Where you went. What you did."

"We just walked around, bought sodas at a small market, and then got some pizza."

"All three of you?"

"Yeah."

"Really? The guy who runs the harbor store where you paid your moorage fee said he spoke with you. You told him that one of your guys was not feeling well and remained below deck."

Terry seemed to pale at Patty's comment. "Why are you concerned about where each of us was? We were at the harbor all day. Your guy should be able to tell you that too. Now, we've got work to do before taking off tomorrow morning. So unless you have a reason to hold us here, we'd like to get on our way."

Patty glanced at Rick. "No problem. We'll ask Officer Bradley to take you back to the reception area. We'll also ask him to bring Arnold back for a few questions. We won't be long."

Terry began to walk away from the table and stopped. "Arnold? He can't help you any more than I did."

Rick got up, walked to the door, and opened it. Brad was waiting in the hall. He escorted Terry back to reception and brought Arnold in for questioning.

It was clear as Arnold sat down that he was much more nervous than Terry had been. He began tapping his foot almost immediately.

Patty started off with the questioning. "Hello, Arnold. Thank you for agreeing to answer a few questions."

"No problem. I don't know anything about a murder, though."

"Who told you there was a murder?"

"Terry did. Well, he didn't say it was a murder, I guess. He said a diver was found."

"Where were you that day?" asked Patty.

Arnold looked up and to his right. Then he stared at his hands. "I was with the other guys."

"And what were they doing?"

"Well, we pretty much stayed on our boat and played cards."

"Oh," said Patty, "Terry must have forgotten about that. He thought you walked around the harbor."

"Yeah, we did that too. Played cards and then walked around the harbor."

"Where did you eat that day?"

"Eat?"

"Yes. Where did you eat lunch or dinner?"

Arnold now looked lost. "I don't remember."

Rick sat forward in his chair. "Let me understand. You and your pals took your boat to Eureka for a couple of days, brought it up to Brookings, then went up to Gold Beach for a day. And you did nothing but walk around? Surely you had some reason to come up the coast. Did Terry have business with someone up this way?"

Arnold wrung his hands on top of the table. "I don't remember."

Rick looked at Patty. "Can we step into the hall a minute?"

Patty followed Rick out the door. "Are you thinking what I'm thinking?"

Rick nodded. "Probably. I'd say they've been on a drug run. A search of their boat would probably corroborate our suspicion, but we don't have cause. A search warrant will take a while."

"They're going to become suspicious very quickly too and get rid of any evidence. We can let them go. I'll call the Coast Guard."

Patty and Rick returned to the interview room.

"Well," said Patty, "that's all the questions we have for now. Thanks for coming in."

Arnold stood up. "Sure. No problem."

Rick walked across the room. He took hold of the door handle and then turned back around toward Arnold. "Have you guys stopped in Brookings before on your trips up the coast?"

Arnold's coloring turned a bit red. "I don't remember."

Rick opened the door. Brad walked Arnold down the hall while Patty and Rick returned to their office.

Rick tapped in a few numbers on his phone. "I'm going to let Mike at the harbor know to keep us informed as to when these guys leave, and if they return."

"While you call Mike, I'll alert the Coasties to our suspicions. They may find reason to board and search the boat."

The office was quiet for a while after the calls. Rick and Patty worked on reports. A little more than an hour had passed when Rick closed his file. "My stomach is telling me it's lunch time. Are you hungry?"

"I could be. Where do you want to go?"

Before Rick could respond, Brad entered the room. "Max Rainy called. He asked if he and Stuart can come in early because Max has to visit his mother this afternoon."

"Sure," said Patty. "Give us an hour."

Brad left and Rick picked up the phone. "I'll order and go pick it up. What do you want?"

Patty pulled a "to go" menu out of her desk drawer.

* * *

Max sat down across from the detectives. "Like I said before, Detectives, I've pretty much told you all I know. Too bad about the dead guy being Jerry. I read in the paper that you found him. Do you know how he died?"

Patty and Rick looked Max in the eyes. "We know," said Patty, "that he probably didn't go out alone. We also know that he told his brother he was going diving with you."

Rick leaned forward. "We know that you and Stuart dove in the same location that the body was found. It's just a matter of time before we find a witness who saw the three of you take your boat out of the harbor."

Max looked surprised. "You think we killed Jerry? No way. What reason would I have to kill him? And besides, Stuart and I weren't out in the boat that day. Have you considered that maybe Jerry went diving alone?"

Patty and Rick glanced at each other and then at Max. "What day?" asked Patty.

Max looked confused. "What do you mean?"

"You just stated that you and Stuart weren't out in the boat the day Jerry was killed. I didn't give you the day Jerry died. So what day was it that you and Stuart were not out in your boat?"

Max paused before responding. "I don't remember."

Rick leaned forward. "You have the look of a guilty man, Max. We'll find out if you were out in your boat and diving the day we believe Jerry was killed. And if you were, we're going to find out if Jerry was with you."

Max dropped his head. "You're barking up the wrong tree, Detectives. If Jerry was murdered, you need to start looking for the guilty party. I'm not a murderer."

Patty glanced at Rick and gave a head nod. They both stood up. Rick walked across the room and opened the door. As Max walked out, Rick commented, "We'll see if Stuart's memory is a little better than yours."

Brad brought Stuart into the room to sit across from the detectives. He nervously looked back and forth at the two detectives and then stared down at his hands.

Patty leaned back in her chair. "You've heard about Jerry's body being found?"

"Yep. That's too bad."

"You've heard he was found at Diver Rock, where you and Max have gone diving many times."

Stuart squirmed in his seat. "Yeah, I heard."

Patty continued. "You lied to us, Stuart. You told us you'd never met Jerry. But you did. You met him the day that you, Max, and Jerry went out in Max's boat."

Stuart momentarily looked startled but maintained his silence.

"You need to tell us the truth, Stuart. We don't believe it was you who murdered Jerry. But if you were there, you're an accessory to the murder, and that means life as you've known it is over."

Stuart looked up at Patty. "I didn't know Jerry, and I don't know anything about his murder."

Rick leaned forward. "What happened out there? Did Max and Jerry get into a fight? Was it an accident? Did Max knock Jerry overboard? You were there, Stuart. Did you push Jerry overboard?"

Stuart stood up. "No. And I'm not going to answer any more questions."

Rick sat back. "Sit down, Stuart. We will find out if Max took his boat out about the time Jerry died. Most likely someone at the harbor or the dock saw you, and we'll find out who that someone is. Then we're going to tie you and Max to Jerry's death. It's only a matter of time."

Stuart sat silently staring at the tabletop. Rick stood up, walked to the door, and asked Brad to take Stuart back to reception.

Back at their desks, Patty and Rick sat quietly working on reports. Patty raised her head. "So, what do you make of Max and Stuart? Neither of them has given us a reason for wanting Jerry dead."

Rick put down his pen and sat back in his chair. "It has to be because we don't yet have enough information. Max comes across as guilty, but there's no way we can tie him to the murder without a motive."

Patty's cell phone vibrated. "O'Toole."

"Hi, Detective. This is PO Heart. How's your day going?"

"PO Heart. It's good to hear from you. My day is going okay, though it would be better if we could solve the murder of our missing diver. How's life treating you?"

"Not bad. Working in parole and probation gives me weekends off with the family. I'm calling because I may have something that will help with your case."

Patty sat up straight in her chair. "Really? That's great. You have my attention."

"It's a knife with the initials J.S. on the handle. The sheath is handmade with the name Stengle stamped into the leather."

"That could certainly have belonged to our victim. Where did you find them?"

"In the backpack of one of my offenders. I found a second knife, along with syringes full of dirty brown liquid, a few pieces of cotton, and a meth cooking spoon."

"You hit the jackpot, Heart. Where was the backpack?"

"With my offender! He came into his appointment with it."

Patty laughed. "He brought his backpack with him to his PO appointment? Sounds like your offender is not the brightest bulb in the room. I guess I'll never get beyond being surprised."

"No, and he's not going to have a chance to get any smarter over the next six months. Deputy Lerange was here and took him up north."

"Did he say where he got the knife?"

"He didn't. But that doesn't mean he doesn't know."

"Does he have any priors?"

"Nothing major. Petty theft and drugs. The small amount of drugs he had on him this time wouldn't have got him in trouble if it weren't for his probation status."

"Got it," said Patty. "Rick and I will give him time for booking and then go up to talk with him. What's his name?"

"Peter Sham. Let me know if he gives up anything. I've already let Detective Finley know about the knife. I'll send photos of it to her and to you."

"Thanks again," said Patty.

Rick looked up from his writing when Patty ended the call. "Heart's offender walked into his appointment with a backpack full of knives and drug paraphernalia. One knife has the initials J.S. on the grip, and the name Stengle stamped onto the leather sheath. She's sending a photo. Let's go interview him after lunch."

Rick nodded. "Sure. I'm glad you want to work lunch in there first."

The detectives worked on their written reports until leaving for the county jail. On the way up Patty commented on the knife. "This guy has a record for petty theft and drugs. It would be a stretch for him to be involved in a murder."

"Unless," said Rick, "he didn't know until it was too late that a murder was to be committed."

The detectives drove to Gold Beach and proceeded downtown to the Sheriff's Office and county jail.

Patty looked out the window as Rick drove. "I like what they've done along here with the decorative benches."

Hearing no response from Rick, Patty spoke again. "The benches. Have you noticed?"

Rick glanced out the window. "Oh, yeah."

"There's also a small, landscaped area with benches in front of the courthouse. It really enhances the aesthetic beauty of the whole downtown area. Don't you think?"

Rick parked on the street in front of the Sheriff's Office. "Yeah. Benches are nice."

The detectives walked into the Sheriff's Office and were greeted by a receptionist. The reception room was small with a photo of the Sheriff on the wall. The Sheriff's Office insignia was on the floor. A young woman sat in an enclosed area behind glass separating her from whomever walked in. She looked up from her desk.

"Detectives O'Toole and Starker. We must be housing someone you want to have a chat with."

"You are, and we do," said Patty. "Peter Sham. He's probably your most recent occupant."

"You are right about that. I'll have him taken to the interview room for you." She buzzed the door, unlocking it for the detectives.

Peter Sham was brought into the room and handcuffed to the metal ring embedded into the table. He sat facing the one-way window. As was their custom, Patty started the questioning while Rick took notes. "Do you know why you're here?"

Sham sat slouched in his chair. "No."

"We're here to talk about the knife and sheath PO Heart found in your backpack. Tell us about that."

"You mean about the knife or PO Heart finding it?"

Patty glanced at Rick and then directed her attention back to Sham. "The knife. Where'd you get it?"

"I found it."

"Where?" asked Patty.

"At the harbor."

"Where at the harbor?"

Sham moved a bit in his chair. He looked around the room and then shifted his gaze to the upper right-hand corner of the room. "Under a picnic table."

Patty responded without pause. "Which table?"

"I don't remember. There are several picnic tables at the harbor. I was just walking along the boardwalk and found the knife."

Patty kept her voice stern. "Well, the boardwalk runs from the ice cream parlor down to the Lucy Dick statue. Whereabouts were you on the boardwalk when you found the knife?"

"I guess I could have been close to the ice cream parlor. Yeah, that was it. I found it under the table closest to the ice cream parlor."

"How did you know Jerry Stengle?"

"Jerry who?"

"Jerry Stengle. It's his knife found in your backpack. How did you know him?"

"I don't know anyone by that name."

Rick opened his file and pulled out a photo of Stengle. He set it in front of Sham.

Patty pointed to the photo. "Think carefully before you speak. Are you sure you don't know this man?"

Sham pushed the photo back toward Rick. "I'm sure."

"Then how is it you have his knife?"

"I told you. I found it under a picnic table. He must have dropped it."

Patty sat back in her chair and Rick continued the questions. "We don't believe you. And I don't think you're taking this conversation seriously, Sham. You had a knife in your possession that belonged to a guy we believe was murdered. That makes you our prime suspect."

Sham sat up. "I didn't kill anyone."

Rick continued. "Who did?"

There was a long pause before Sham answered. "I don't know."

"Then tell us where you got the knife."

Sham shook his head. "I can't."

Patty took over and Rick sat back. "Why not?"

Sham squirmed in his chair. "Because I just can't."

Patty softened her voice. "Is it because of what Max Rainy will do to you if he finds out?"

Sham jerked up in his seat. "I didn't say it was Max."

"So you do know Max."

Sham began looking back and forth between Patty and Rick. "No. I mean, I've heard his name."

"Have you been fishing with him?"

Sham shook his head. "No. I told you I don't know him."

Patty continued to speak in a sympathetic tone. "We know you don't want to go to prison, Peter. There are a lot of things you still want to do in life. Things that you won't be able to do if you go to prison. You are already facing six months in jail for being on probation and having drugs in your possession. Do you have any idea what will happen to a young guy like you if you spend the next twenty years living with guys twice your size? So tell me, Peter, where did you get the knife?"

Sham's eyes filled with tears. "He'll kill me if I tell on him. I'm not saying anything else. I found the knife under a picnic table."

Patty glanced at Rick. "I think Mr. Sham needs to contemplate what his future in prison will be like. We're done with you for now, Sham. But we'll be back after we talk with Max."

Sham's tone turned to anger. "You can tell him anything you want. He knows I don't talk to cops."

Patty and Rick left the jail and started back to Brookings. "So," said Patty, "we've got another possible suspect. Do you think he could have been involved in Jerry's murder?"

"Hard to tell yet if he was involved. But I think he knows about it. He definitely knows Max."

"I agree," said Patty. "Let's talk with Max and see how he reacts to Sham's name and the knife."

Patty called Brad and asked that he bring Max in for questioning the following morning. "If he has an excuse for not coming in, let him know we'll be at his place tomorrow morning at nine, and we'll expect to see him there." Patty ended the call. "It seems our mild-mannered Max Rainy isn't the friendly fellow he would like us to believe he is. We've got to find a way to get one of these guys to talk."

CHAPTER ELEVEN

The portable radio squawked, and the detectives heard dispatch describe a bank robbery in progress. "All units respond. There's an active bank robbery at the downtown branch of River City Credit Union. Robber is wearing a bright yellow down jacket and jeans. He left the bank walking south on Chetco."

Several units responded and, with cars lit up and sirens blaring, approached the bank from several directions. The radio squawked and a second call came through. "All units, the Northwest Bank on Chetco has been robbed by the same suspect. He's last seen walking southwest toward Railroad Avenue." Several units responded again.

"Shall we go find the guy?" asked Rick.

"Sure," said Patty. "Let's drive down Fifth to Railroad."

Three minutes later, the car radio squawked again. "All units be advised. The suspect is in custody at the corner of Railroad and Cove. Repeat. Suspect has been apprehended."

Rick pulled up to the curb of the local restaurant on the corner described by dispatch. They could see a patrol officer and a young man standing over a guy in a yellow jacket. The man in the yellow jacket was seated and drinking a cup of coffee.

"Need some help?" asked Patty.

"No, I think we've got this," said the officer.

"How'd you find him so quickly?" asked Rick.

The officer pointed to the young man next to him. "He spotted him. Danny is an Explorer Scout on a ride-along with me today. I'm new to Brookings and not yet familiar with all the side streets. Danny here was a great help guessing where the suspect was headed. We responded to the call and drove first to the Credit Union. From there we drove to Northwest Bank and learned that the suspect had just left. So, we turned onto Railroad, and Danny pointed in front of us. 'That's him!' he said. Well, I was looking around closer to the car and asked, 'Where?' Danny pointed again. 'Right there. The man with the yellow jacket.'

"Then I saw him. Just sitting here drinking a cup of coffee. I was just about to cuff him when you showed up. I've asked for a couple of officers to bring a witness from each of the banks on a drive-by to see whether they can identify him as the guy who robbed their bank. We'll take him in after he's ID'd." The officer pulled several bundles of bills from the man's pockets and laid them on the table. "We'll need a bag for this money."

"I'll get one out of the trunk," said Rick.

Patty looked down at the man sitting quietly at the table sipping his coffee. "What's your name?"

The man slowly took his wallet out of his pocket and opened it to show his driver's license.

Patty looked at the license. "Doug Street?"

The man nodded in the affirmative.

She gave the man's wallet back to him. He put it in the pocket of his yellow jacket, never lifting his eyes from the ground. The quiet was interrupted when the Scout asked, "Why did you do it?"

The man looked up at the young man. "To see if I could."

Patty and Rick stayed with the officer, Scout, and suspect until the suspect was identified by a witness from each of the two banks and taken to the station.

Patty and Rick returned to their office. Rick stopped at the break room and, thirty seconds later, entered the office with a cupcake in one hand and a cup of coffee in the other. "Not much more we can do today. Did Brad say whether he got ahold of Max?"

Patty nodded. "Our appointment is at nine and it's here."

"Okay. I'll be in about eight. See you then."

"I'll be leaving soon myself. See ya."

Rick found himself drawn to the AA meeting, not because he needed it tonight but because he hoped to see Stella. He sat in his usual place in the back of the room.

An hour and a half later, the meeting ended. He left for home. Stella hadn't shown.

* * *

Patty arrived at the office at eight and found Rick writing up a report.

"Good morning. I've got a chocolate old-fashioned doughnut for me and a lemon-filled pastry for you if you want it."

Rick looked up. "I do. Thanks."

Patty put a napkin down on the corner of Rick's desk and set the pastry on top of it.

"This morning I looked at the weather report for the weekend and it's supposed to rain. Ever consider how unfair it is at times when we have beautiful days like today during the work week and then a weekend of rain?"

"No. I just figure *it is what it is.* The rain doesn't bother me."

"Well, I guess you're right. But there are times of the year when it's difficult to plan anything outside because one day it can be overcast and misty at fifty-three degrees, and the next might be a warm sixty-one with no wind. The following day can be cloudy and fifty-eight with eight- to fifteen-mile-per-hour winds." Patty waited for Rick's response.

"That's why it's always good to have a plan B."

Patty smiled and hung her jacket on the back of her chair. "Have you given any thought on how to approach Max?"

Rick chewed on a bite of pastry. Patty waited for him to swallow. He picked up his napkin and wiped the lemon filling off the side of his lip.

"What do we know about the man? He's a diver, and among his friends and acquaintances he's a big fish in a little pond. He hangs out with guys who have little ambition and even less sense. He has opportunity and the means to have committed the murder. What we haven't come up with yet is a motive, and that is bothersome. We've interviewed four guys who either hang out or used to hang out with him. Stuart, Connor, Trevor, and now Peter Sham. None of them seem to have a reason for wanting Jerry Stengle dead, and all but Max and Stuart have an alibi for the estimated day of death."

Patty tapped her pencil on her desk. "They all seem to have some fear of Max, leading me to believe that he's the most likely to be able to kill. So what are we hoping to achieve with this morning's interview?"

"We can ask him about the knife, but what I'd like to do at this point is get him riled up. I want him to know that we know he can get angry." Rick took another bite of his pastry. "How about you?" he asked while still chewing.

"I want to ask him more questions about his relationship with Jerry. All we've been told thus far is that he knew Jerry in high school but only as a fellow student. I want to know if there's more to their relationship."

Brad stepped up to the office door. "Max is here. He knows he's early. Do you want to see him now or have him wait until nine?"

Patty glanced at Rick who popped that last bit of pastry in his mouth, took a sip of coffee, and stood up. She looked up at Brad. "Looks like we'll interview him now."

In the interview room, Max sat, looking sure of himself. He leaned back in the metal chair with his arms crossed over his chest.

"Hello again, Max. Detective Starker and I appreciate your coming in. We've got some new information that has brought about additional questions for you."

Max maintained his position. "New information?"

Rick put the photo of the knife and sheath in front of Max.

"Yes," said Patty. "Do you recognize this knife?"

Max brought the chair back to rest on all four legs and sat up. "Why should I know whose knife that was?"

"'Was'? That sounds like you know who it belonged to. It sounds as though you think the owner of the knife is dead."

"Well, I can read the name Stengle on the sheath, and you brought me in to talk about your case. So I assumed it belonged to Jerry Stengle." Max took on a troubled look, creasing his forehead as he spoke.

"You have a question?" Patty asked.

Max shook his head. "Not really. I was just wondering where you got it. Did Jerry have it on him when you found the body?"

"No," Patty said. "And I think you know where we got the knife." She glanced at Rick who leaned forward. "We got it from your friend, Peter Sham."

Hearing Sham's name caused Max to turn pale. His left eye began to twitch. Rick continued.

"We've been talking with your buddy, Sham. He told us about the knife."

Patty took over the questioning with a softened tone. "We know you gave that knife to Peter Sham, Max. Did you take it from Jerry before you killed him?"

Max started shaking his head.

Patty increased the volume of her voice. "Did Sham see you kill Jerry? Did you give Sham the knife in exchange for his silence?"

Max's head movement became more erratic. "No, no, no!"

Rick stood, leaned over the table, and yelled at Max. "Why'd you do it, Max? Why'd you kill Jerry Stengle?"

"I didn't kill anyone," yelled Max.

Patty spoke softly. "What did he do to you, Max, to make you so angry that you wanted him dead?"

Max's eyes became large. He slammed the palms of his hands on the table and looked back and forth from Patty to Rick. His complexion became dark red. Then, as though he'd cleared his mind and refocused on what was happening, he sat down and spoke quietly again.

"I didn't kill anyone and I'm not answering any more of your questions. You're going to have to either arrest me or leave me alone."

The detectives stood up, and Patty stared at Max. "We know there's a lot you're not telling us, Max. We will find Jerry's killer, and if it's you, you'll go away for a long, long time."

Brad escorted Max to the reception area. Patty and Rick walked back to their office.

Rick thumbed through his notes. "This is a tough one, Patty. Even if we get one of the others to say Max killed Jerry, we have no evidence. He'd never be convicted of murder. We don't even have enough for a search warrant."

Patty's cell phone rang, and she looked up at Rick. "It's Doc Miller."

"Hey, Doc. Great to hear from you."

The doc laughed. "Hi, Patty. Is it great because you want to know how busy my life is, or because you want to learn your diver's cause of death?"

"Both," said Patty. "Rick is here, so I've got you on speaker."

Rick made his presence known. "Hi, Doc."

"Hi, Rick. You and Patty sure know how to find the not-so-common cases."

Rick smiled. "Guess we're lucky that way, Doc."

"Well, to answer Patty's question, life is busy as always. But I'm calling to let you know why your diver didn't drop his vest and swim to the surface, and why it's taken this long for me to get back to you."

"Was he dead before hitting the water?"

"No. There was water in his lungs indicating he was still alive. But he was incapacitated with a drug called succinylcholine."

Patty struggled with the name. "That's a new one for me, Doc."

"Well, Patty, it's not heard of much because it's awfully hard to get ahold of the drug outside of a hospital. Succinylcholine is hard to detect. We wouldn't have looked for a drug if a thorough autopsy hadn't been performed. The key was finding the needle hole between his fingers. The autopsy has now identified what was injected, but it's not because we found the drug itself in his system."

"Can you explain that for us, Doc?" asked Rick.

"The drug is one that is used in surgery to relax the muscles. Its use results in skeletal muscle paralysis. It's a depolarizing neuromuscular blocker and is difficult to detect because its metabolites are all naturally-occurring molecules.

However, testing can be done on the metabolites, which are the breakdown products resulting from succinylcholine being metabolized by the body.

"Testing in this manner has proved successful in many cases. There's a famous homicide case in which the doctor was able to isolate one of the metabolites of succinylcholine called succinic acid. The doctor found large quantities of this acid in the brain tissues of the victim."

The doctor's explanation left Patty and Rick silent.

Doc Miller laughed. "That's a lot to take in, I know."

"You're not kidding, Doc," said Rick.

"So, Doc," said Patty, "is this something that he would have drunk before going into the water?"

"No. Succinylcholine is not taken orally. It's injected. It was injected between Jerry's fingers. This means that whoever killed Jerry first put enough peanut oil on his mouthpiece to cause anaphylactic shock. Then the killer injected succinylcholine, which instantly paralyzed Jerry, leaving him no way to swim to the surface."

Rick exhaled. "So we're looking for someone who either works for a hospital or obtained this drug illegally."

"I'd say that's a good description, Rick. It won't be easy, but I know that you and Patty will work it out."

"Thanks, Doc," said Patty.

"Yeah, Doc," said Rick. "Thanks for your confidence."

"You're welcome. Let me know how it goes."

"Will do," said Patty.

Patty ended the call and looked at Rick. "This isn't a crime of passion."

"No," said Rick. "It took skill and premeditation. If we can connect that drug with Max, we'll have him."

Patty nodded. "So let's find evidence of the drug being used. Why don't you check with the hospitals and find out if they've any record of a theft of the drug? I'll go online and find out who makes it."

Rick's cell phone rang, and it took him a few seconds to recognize the number before answering. "Stella?"

"Hi, Rick. Hope I'm not interrupting anything."

"No. I'm at work, but I can talk. How are you?"

"I'm okay. How about you?"

"Yeah. I'm okay too. I've missed you at the meetings."

"Yeah, well, that's kind of what I'm calling about."

Rick glanced up at Patty, who quickly looked back down at her report. He responded to Stella's comment with reluctance. "Oh?"

"Yeah, well, I… I like you, Rick. I like you a lot even though we've only just met. I found it difficult to sleep for a couple of nights after our dinner, thinking of getting closer to you and worrying about that very same thing." Stella paused.

"Stella, I think I understand. I like you too. That's why we decided to move forward slowly with our relationship."

"I know, Rick. But I'm just not ready for a relationship, not even a slow one."

"Did I say or do something that made you feel uncomfortable?"

"Oh, no, Rick. Nothing at all. I guess that's part of the problem. You're a great guy. But it hasn't been long enough for me since my divorce. I'm not even two years sober. I'm just beginning to learn who I am, and I need to spend more time on getting to know me before I enter a relationship with anyone else."

Rick was surprised and disappointed so it took him a few minutes to recover.

"Are you there, Rick?"

"I'm here. You need to do whatever you think is necessary, Stella, to stay strong and sober. I understand that. Maybe we can just be friends for a while. See where that takes us."

The line was silent again.

Rick moved the phone away from his ear and then brought it back again. "Now it's my turn to ask. Are you there?"

"I'm moving, Rick."

"Moving? Where?"

"Back to Texas. I'm moving in with my sister until I find a place of my own. I already have a job lined up so that I'll work close to home, my sister, and her family. I'm sorry, Rick."

"No, no. Don't be sorry, Stella. I'm sure you've given a lot of thought to this, and you need to do what's right for you. I understand."

"Thanks, Rick. If I send you a letter now and then, will you respond?"

"Well, sure. I'm not much of a letter-writer, though. So you'll have to be patient. But I would appreciate your letting me know that you're okay."

"I will. Well, bye, Rick. I'm glad I met you."

"Yeah, me too. Take care, Stella."

Rick set the phone down, sat back in his chair, and stared at his desk.

Patty put down her pen. "You okay?"

Rick looked up. "I will be."

"You want to talk about it?"

"Maybe. But not now. Right now I'm going to research hospitals that keep succinylcholine on hand."

Patty nodded. The quiet of the room was deafening until Brad walked through the door. "We've got a lost child in the woods around Agness. Call from the father just came in. We've alerted the Sheriff, and he's coordinating SAR. He's asking for assistance now, knowing it will take thirty to sixty minutes for help to get there."

Patty and Rick closed their respective files, put on their jackets, and left the office.

"Let me get my emergency pack out of my trunk," said Patty.

Rick drove, and thirty-five minutes later they were in Gold Beach turning off onto Jerry's Flat Road. The car radio provided an updated status report. "To all responding to the call for SAR members, report to Sargent Hogram at the Singing Springs Resort Restaurant. The child was last seen by her ten-year-old brother an hour and a half ago. No one thought of her as missing until he was asked to bring her to the restaurant for dinner and couldn't find her. That was thirty minutes ago. Her parents reported her missing. She's eight years old, is wearing jeans, a pink t-shirt, green windbreaker, and pink tennis shoes."

Patty responded over the radio. "This is Detectives O'Toole and Starker.

We've just turned onto Jerry's Flat Road. We'll go directly to the restaurant unless otherwise advised."

Rick slowed down for another hairpin turn. "I've got to say that, after hearing the SAR talk for the Scouts, I feel confident that the little girl will be located. She couldn't have gone too far."

Patty stared out the window. "I hope not."

Rick slowed down for another sharp turn. "This road's had some work since we last drove it. Nice not to have to dodge so many large potholes."

"I think it probably requires constant work. Like Hooskanaden, the land seems to always be moving."

Rick pulled into the Singing Springs parking lot. They grabbed their emergency packs out of the trunk and entered the restaurant. Sergeant Hogram was speaking with a half-dozen SAR members while pointing to a map. He recognized the detectives and nodded, then he finished giving instructions and summarized.

"So what have we done thus far? Upon learning the child was missing, we activated a call out to CORSAR. We've already secured the PLS or Point Last Seen. We've requested an air-scent trailing dog and a man-tracker. Both the dog and the man-tracker should be here within the next thirty minutes. The Marine Patrol has responded. They are already searching along the river. SAR Coordinator Waring will be your lead. He has a radio and will share communications with you.

"You each have a whistle. Use it if you see anything that suggests the child may have come through your area. This means inspecting both the ground for footprints and bushes for broken twigs. If any of you take the man-tracking courses, you'll learn that even bruised leaves and grass can tell a story about where someone has walked. Footprints tell us shoe size. You'll be searching a designated area on the map for about five hours. Any questions?"

Hearing none, he finished, "I'll ask you all to follow the deputy out the side door."

The sergeant turned toward Patty and Rick. "Thanks for coming out, Detectives. Detective Finley is on vacation, and I need to have the family members questioned." He turned toward the deputy working on paperwork at the front counter. "Have the group of non-SAR volunteers take a seat and wait for me. I'll be at the back table with the detectives."

The sergeant turned toward the detectives. "We always have private citizens who want to search," he said, "but we often can't allow it. We've got to protect the area from contamination that might make it impossible to see footprints and other signs integral to finding our missing person."

"I understand," said Patty.

"Sergeant," said Rick, "can you remind me what CORSAR means?"

"Sure. It's an acronym for California Oregon Regional Search and Rescue Task Force."

The sergeant led Patty and Rick to a table in the back of the outdoor seating area.

"Here's what we've got. The eight-year-old missing girl arrived here on a jet boat with her mom, stepdad, and ten-year-old brother. They are from eastern Oregon. The last time any of them saw the girl was about three-thirty this afternoon when the boat docked. They all walked up the ramp together. The girl and her brother split from the parents and went over to play on the lawn. We're searching the woods around the resort and along the river. She's been missing one and a half to two hours, depending on whether she was still in the immediate area for a while after her brother last saw her."

Rick took some notes while Patty looked around at some of the visitors waiting to learn the news.

"Have you asked the parents any questions?" she asked.

"Only about timing. When and where they last saw their daughter."

"Where can we sit with them?"

Sergeant Hogram pointed to one of the tables. "You can have this table. I've got to put together another volunteer search group. If you're ready to begin interviewing, I'll bring the parents to you."

Patty took a seat. "I want to start with the mother. What are their names?"

The sergeant looked at his notes. "Thomas and Candace Palmer."

"Okay. We'll talk first with Candace."

Patty watched as Hogram walked across the room to a table where the family sat waiting. Both parents looked dazed and frightened. Candace stood up, looked at Patty, and joined her and Rick at their table.

Patty was careful to lead into the conversation gently. "Hi, Candace. I'm Detective O'Toole and this is Detective Starker. We're sorry to learn that your daughter's missing."

Candace nodded as the tears began rolling down an already mascara-stained face. Her swollen eyes and red nose expressed her grief before she spoke. She clinched a wad of tissue in the palm of one hand.

"We need to ask you a few questions, Candace. If I ask anything you don't want to answer, just let me know. Okay?"

The young mother nodded and then uttered a quiet plea. "Please find her."

Patty continued. "The sheriff's office and volunteers are working hard to do just that. What is your daughter's full name?"

"Tina Marie Johnson."

"That's a beautiful name," said Patty. "Your husband must be Tina's step-father. I notice the different last name. Is that right?"

"Yes, but he's her dad as far as our family is concerned. I married Thomas when Tina was three years old. We've been planning for him to adopt the kids so that we all will carry the Palmer name."

"I see," said Patty. "And your son's name?"

"His name is Scott William Johnson."

"When did you last see your daughter?"

"When we arrived on the jet boat."

"What was she doing and wearing when you last saw her?"

Candace paused. "She ran off with her brother to play. They saw the lawn area where a few other kids were playing. I called out to them not to leave the area because we'd be eating soon." Candace gave Patty a dazed look. "What was your other question?"

"Not a problem. I asked what Tina was wearing?"

"Oh. She had on her pink t-shirt, blue jeans, and a green jacket. She has her pink tennis shoes on. I think she put her green socks on today too." Candace smiled slightly as she described her daughter's outfit. "She always looks so pretty in pink and green."

Patty smiled. "Now, Candace, I want to ask a few questions that will require your full concentration. It might help for you to close your eyes. Where have you been since stepping off the boat?"

Candace looked at Patty. "I don't need to close my eyes. Thomas and I walked up here to the restaurant and sat down. We talked until Scott came in for a drink of water. Thomas asked him to get his sister and let her know it's time for dinner."

"Where did you sit?" asked Patty

Candace pointed to another table. "Right there."

"You and Thomas sat down together. Did you stay together at that table during the time Tina and Scott were away from you?"

"Yes. Well, we each went to the bathroom, but other than that, we've been here." Candace blew her nose. She then shook her head and looked first at Patty and then to Rick. "Why are you asking about Thomas and me? My daughter is alone out there. Shouldn't you be looking for her?"

Patty looked toward Rick, and he spoke to Candace. "We'll do everything we can to help, but Sergeant Hogram is a SAR Coordinator. He's running the search, and he's asked us to remain here for now. Mrs. Palmer, is there anyone else on this boat trip that you and Thomas know? Friends or neighbors?"

"No. It's just us." She looked across the room at her husband.

Rick continued. "Is Tina a child who might simply run off on her own? For instance, if she saw a butterfly or a deer, would she be apt to wander into the woods following it?"

"Oh, yes. Tina is very inquisitive. And she has no fear. She's never been afraid, at least not until now. She's out there somewhere, lost and alone." The distraught mother looked at Rick. "They will find her, won't they?"

"Sergeant Hogram and others on the Sheriff's Search and Rescue team are very capable. They know how to navigate the river and these woods. They've done this many, many times before."

Patty thanked Candace and asked her to please go back to where she'd been seated and let her husband know that the detectives would like to ask him a few questions. Thomas stood after his wife returned to their table, walked over to Patty and Rick, and sat down. His face was one of pained expression. His brows were tightly drawn as though he were deep in thought.

"What is it you want to know, Detectives?"

Patty introduced herself and Rick. "We're sorry that your daughter's missing. We know this is a very difficult time for you and your wife."

"My wife won't survive this if Tina isn't found. We've only been married about five years. Candace, Tina, and Scott are the only real family I've ever had. We can't lose Candace. Do you understand?"

Patty spoke softly. "Search and Rescue are doing all they can, and they are the best at what they do. Please walk us through your actions once you left the boat."

"My actions? The four of us walked up the path. Then the kids took off toward the lawn where we could hear other children playing. Candace and I came into the restaurant, sat down at the table, and talked."

"Did either of you leave the table during that time?"

"Only to use the bathroom. And I bought us each a glass of wine."

"Can you describe what Tina was wearing this morning?"

Thomas was quiet for a few seconds. "Well, she had on her blue jeans and a jacket. I think it was green. She had a pink shirt on too. I don't pay a lot of attention to what the kids wear every day. Candace helps them with their clothes."

Before Patty could go on, Sergeant Hogram walked quickly into the restaurant and up to the table where the detectives and Thomas were sitting. He looked over at Candace. She saw him enter and stood up. Thomas walked across the room and protectively put his arm around his wife.

Hogram glanced at the detectives and then looked at the parents. "We found her."

Candace let out a brief high-pitched scream. "Is she alright?"

Thomas held his wife closer, helping her to remain on her feet.

"We'll need to have her seen by a physician, but it appears that, other than a possible sprained ankle, a few scrapes, and some bug bites, she's fine."

"Where is she?" asked Candace.

"She was found by two SAR members in the woods not far from here. She evidently tripped and fell, hurting her ankle, then was unable to get up. We're bringing her out on a stretcher so as not to risk further damage to the ankle."

Candace stood up quickly. "Will they bring her here? I need to see her."

"We'll bring her in here to see you both before she's taken by boat back to the port. We all just need to wait patiently until she's brought in."

Fifteen minutes later, Tina was brought into the room on a stretcher. Seeing her parents, she quickly sat upright. "Mommy! Dad!"

Candace ran up to her daughter and hugged her. "Are you hurting?"

Tina looked at her mother. "Just my ankle. I fell over a tree limb. And my arm itches where some bugs bit me. Why are you crying, Mommy?"

"I'm just so happy, Tina. We were all scared something horrible had happened to you. Why did you go into the forest?"

A smile came to Tina's face. "I followed a squirrel. He was a fuzzy one with a big tail. Then I fell. I called out, but no one could hear me, so I figured I'd just wait for Scott to come get me when it was dinner time."

Sergeant Hogram announced that two EMTs were ready to take Tina down to the rescue boat and back to the port.

Thomas put his arm around his wife's shoulders. "Can Candace go with Tina?"

"That will be fine," said Hogram. "A pilot will transport you and Scott back to the port so that you can pick up your car and drive to Curry General Hospital."

Thomas thanked the sergeant and then turned to the owner of Singing Springs Resort. "You and your employees have been very kind. Please give our appreciation to all of them."

Patty and Rick thanked Hogram and left for their office. Once in the car, Patty turned to Rick. "I wish they could all end like that."

Rick started the engine. "Yeah, I do too. This will give the Sheriff's SAR volunteers enough adrenalin to keep their spirits lifted for some time."

Patty smile. "Let's hope we have as much success with our murdered diver as the Sheriff's SAR team has experienced with this search."

CHAPTER TWELVE

Thirty minutes later the detectives were turning off Jerry's Flat Road onto Ellensburg Avenue. Patty pointed to the Gold Beach Bookstore as they passed. "Have you been in the bookstore lately?"

"I have not. Is it different?"

"To say that it's different is an understatement. The first floor is totally changed. There are now beautiful sculptures sitting upon antique tables where bookshelves were. There is also a selection of glass art and paintings, including some by local artists. When I was last there, the new books I saw on the main floor included those by some of our local authors. All used books are now upstairs."

"I'll have to check it out when I have time."

The detectives became quiet as they traveled south on Highway 101. Patty pointed to their left as they passed Whaleshead Resort, a development of park-model homes tightly hugging the side of a hill with views across the highway to the ocean. "The owners of that development own the land and collect land-lease fees from the park-model owners. Though the homeowners don't own the land on which their homes sit, they do have beautiful views."

Rick glanced up the hill. "I can see that, but it's not my idea of home. I don't need a big house, but I do want several acres of land around me."

"I know you do, Rick. And much of the land here in Curry County is beautiful. At this time of year, the forest trees are stunning with the sun shining through their branches. Much different than it is in the winter, when the smoke curls through the trees and across the highway."

"Murder on the wind," said Rick. "That's what you called the curling smoke."

Patty laughed. "Yes, and there was murder on the wind when I made that comment. That was a great solve we made, with the assistance of the Sheriff and other members of our major crimes team."

"I enjoyed that," said Rick. "I remain in touch with one of the Washington State Patrol troopers I met on that case."

Patty looked across the center console at Rick. "We've worked well together, Rick. I'm not sure I could have solved those cases without you." Patty paused before continuing. "Your coming back to Brookings has made a big difference in my life."

Rick smiled. "It feels good to be back working with you, Patty. I'm glad I left when I did, though. It's hard to explain, but losing my wife and daughter shattered everything I knew and believed about my life and my future. All I could do was go on living until I felt alive again.

"You helped me do that for the first several years, but I just wanted time to straighten a few things out in my mind. And I needed to leave Brookings to accomplish what was necessary. I realized today, taking this drive again with you to work on a case, how much I missed our teamwork."

The air was silent as Rick pulled into the police department parking lot.

Patty jumped when her cell phone rang. "It's Mom," she said out loud to Rick. "I'll catch up with you in the office." She tapped on the phone. "Detective O'Toole."

"Hello, Detective O'Toole. This is your mother."

"Hi, Mom. How's your day going?"

"I'm fine, dear. Bill and I just got back. We took Oscar for a walk."

"I'll bet Oscar loved that. Where did you go?"

"Oh, just around the block. Bill tires quickly nowadays, and Oscar doesn't like walking for more than about thirty minutes. How's your day going?"

"Rick and I have just returned from a search and rescue effort in Agness. A child had gone missing. Two of the Sheriff's SAR members found her."

"Oh, Patty. That's a terrifying experience. How is the child?"

"She's okay. A possible sprained ankle and some scratches. She'll be fine. To tell you the truth, I think the ordeal may have been much harder on her parents."

"That could be the case since the child wasn't hurt badly, Patty. Parents of missing children suffer greatly during the time their child is gone. I'm happy for you, Rick, and all the others involved that the child was found. On the topic of Agness, are the jet boats running now?"

"They are. How's your friend?"

"You mean Grace? She's good. She is a joy for me to be around because she is so funny at times. Whenever we've been together and she starts talking, she uses phrases that she learned from her mother growing up, not knowing what many of them mean."

"You mean phrases like 'fair-to-middling'?"

Maggie laughed. "Yes. Do you know what that means?"

"Of course I do, Mom. I'm not going to use a phrase I don't understand. It means 'so-so.'"

"Right. Now, what about the phrase, 'sweatin' like a turk'?"

Patty laughed. "I think I may have heard you use that phrase a few times. It must have an Irish origin."

"It does. The word 'turk' in Ireland was used to describe a brawny laborer. And, yes, I'm sure I've used it now and then as I can remember your grandmother using it every time she became overheated."

"I'm happy for you to have such a fun friend, Mom. You'll have to share with her the Irish phrase I used to beg you to say to me when I was little. Do you remember?"

"Do I remember? I teased you with it, but it wasn't used for teasing when I was a child. 'It's the back of me hand you'll be get'n if you don't be behave'n yourself.'"

Patty and Maggie both laughed as Maggie offered the phrase with a strong Irish accent.

"Well, I'm going to let you go," said Maggie. "It's good to hear you laugh, dear."

"Good to laugh with you, Mom. Thanks for sharing your humor."

"Love you, Patty."

"Love you too, Mom."

Patty entered the office to find Rick at his computer researching hospitals that stocked succinylcholine. Patty sat down at her computer to continue her research on how the drug is marketed. She sat back in her chair and rubbed her eyes. "How are you doing?"

Rick put his pen down. "Succinylcholine is kept in locked cabinets in several hospitals across the northwest. Everyone I've spoken with about it swears it's impossible to steal the drug out of the hospital. However, there is a hospital in Eureka that has a record of two vials of the drug that went missing eight years ago. They were never recovered."

"Eight years ago? That's a long time for someone to keep the drug for whatever use they had in mind."

"Unless," said Rick, "the reason for stealing the drug ceased to exist, and the thief decided to hold onto it rather than throw it out. What about you? Find out who sells it?"

"Yes. The brand names are Quelicin and Anectine, and it's sold at several pharmacies. A prescription would be required for purchase. Which means that we're no closer to coming up with Max's source for the drug than when we started."

Rick sat back and folded his arms over his chest. "I still feel strongly that we need to search Max's house. I just don't know how we're going to come up with a reason that will justify a warrant."

"We've been in this position before, Rick. Something will break."

"I know. You're right. It's just a matter of time. Let's talk again with Peter Sham. Now that he's spent several days in jail, he might be more willing to tell us why he's afraid of Max."

Patty reached for the phone. "If Max is as tough a guy as I'm beginning to think he is, jail may be easier for Peter than whatever Max has threatened him with. I'll ask Brad to set it up."

Patty spoke with Brad and then looked at Rick as he quietly worked on his report. "Want to talk about Stella?"

Rick looked up. "There's really not much to say. I knew when we went out that there was danger in dating someone who has only been sober for fifteen months. I guess I liked the comfort of being with someone who understands what it takes to maintain a life of sobriety."

There was a moment of quiet before Patty responded. "I can understand that. We all feel most comfortable when we're with people who have similar lifestyles to our own. Familiarity can make us feel safe."

"Yeah, well, I don't know about that, but I did feel comfortable with Stella. And I like feeling comfortable. Dating at my age is a bear!"

"Rick?"

"Yeah."

"Do you feel comfortable with me?"

Rick leaned back a bit and cocked his head to the side as though he was surprised at the question. "Of course I do. I trust you completely and I know you've always got my back."

The corners of Patty's mouth lifted to a small smile.

"Well, that's not exactly what I'm asking."

"Oh? What are you asking?"

Patty moved around in her chair. "Well, I'm not a recovering alcoholic, and I enjoy a glass of wine most evenings. Does that make you uncomfortable to be with me outside of the job?"

"No. Not at all. Dating Barbara didn't make me uncomfortable either, and she enjoyed an evening drink. So, no. Your having a drink when we're together doesn't make me feel uncomfortable."

Patty and Rick looked into each other's eyes.

"That's good," Patty said. "Because I want you to ask me again to have dinner with you, and this time I'll make it. And I'll include a glass of wine with my meal."

"Okay. When?"

"Tomorrow night."

Rick picked up his cell phone. "I'll have to check my calendar, but I think I'm free."

Patty shook her head and smiled. Rick thumbed through the pages on his phone. "Looks like I'm free. Tomorrow night we'll go to dinner after work."

CHAPTER THIRTEEN

The interview with Peter Sham was at nine A.M.

"How do you want to do this?" Rick asked.

Patty responded without hesitation. "Good cop, bad cop, and you start."

Rick walked into the room first. "Good morning, Peter."

Sham was seated behind a metal table where his handcuffs were secured to a large metal ring.

"Hi."

"How do you like being a guest of the state?"

"I don't. And I've got nothing to say to you."

Rick leaned back in his chair. "Well, that's no way to start off a conversation. Especially when we're here to offer you something a little more comfortable."

Sham looked at Rick. "What do you mean?"

Rick pulled a small card out of his pocket. "Before we go any further, I'm going to read you your rights."

"I've heard them," said Sham.

Rick ignored the remark and continued. "You have the right to remain silent. Anything you say can and will be used against you in a court of law. You have the right to talk to a lawyer and have him present with you while you are being questioned. If you cannot afford to hire a lawyer, one will be appointed to represent you before any questioning if you wish. You can decide at any time to exercise these rights and not answer any questions or make any statements. Do you understand each of these rights I have explained to you?"

Sham moved his head up and down.

"I need a yes or a no."

Sham sighed. "Yes."

Rick continued. "Having these rights in mind, do you wish to talk to us now?"

"Sure, I'll talk to you."

"You look tired, Peter. Your eyes are framed in dark circles, and the skin under both eyes is sagging in layers. You look like you've aged ten years since being locked up. Are you not sleeping?"

Sham remained silent.

"I mean," Rick continued, "that it's clear looking at you that you're not sleeping well. And you've got more than five months to go before you see the outside world again. That's almost half a year. Maybe we can find a way to speed up your return to life on the outside. Is that of any interest to you?"

Sham slumped in his chair. "How can you do that?"

"Tell us why you're scared of Max Rainy. We know he gave you Jerry's knife and sheath. Why? Was it to keep you quiet? What did you see, Peter? Did you see Max kill Jerry Stengle?"

At the mention of Max and Jerry, Sham stiffened and jerked his handcuffs against the ring. "I told you I won't talk about Max. I know what you're trying to do. It won't work."

Patty leaned forward and Rick sat back. She spoke softly. "Peter, we don't know what Max has threatened to do to you, but if we can put him away, he won't be able to hurt you anymore. You'll be able to live without fear. Don't you want that?"

Peter's head seemed to hang in defeat. "You can't put Max away. And he'll still be out there when I get out."

Patty raised her voice. "Don't you want to get out of here? Aren't you afraid of the other prisoners?"

Peter brought his head up and looked into Patty's eyes. "Yes, I'm afraid, but I'm a lot more afraid of Max and what he'll do to me if I talk." He turned toward the door. "Guard!"

The prisoner's cuffs were released from the iron ring, and he was escorted back to his cell.

Rick and Patty walked to their car. Once inside, Patty followed up on the interview. "This validates for us that Max has a hold on Peter and, I suspect, Stuart."

Rick pulled out of the county parking. "I agree. Let's talk to Connor and Trevor again. Their comments suggested that Max was to be feared, but they didn't seem as close to Max as Peter or Stuart. Maybe we can get them to talk about why they don't know Max better. Maybe there's history."

"When we're back at the office, I'll call and ask if they'll meet us in Brookings. I'll suggest they make a fishing day out of it."

Patty's cell phone rang on the drive back to Brookings. "It's Becky," she said to Rick before taking the call. "Hi, Bec."

"Hi, Mom. Got time to talk?"

"I do, but Rick and I are on our way back to Brookings from the jail. I'm going to lose the cell connection in about twenty minutes. I'll call back from the office if that happens."

"No problem, Mom. I don't need twenty minutes. As you know, I volunteer for an organization that helps abandoned animals by restoring their health and finding loving homes. We hold a fundraiser every year, and this year it's a golf tournament. You mentioned years ago that you took golf lessons, so I'm hoping you'll join my team."

"I did take lessons a few decades ago, but I only played one game. It was eighteen holes and seemed to take all day. I didn't have time to play golf then, and I haven't played since."

"Well, okay, Mom. If you really don't want to help me out. This would involve one nine-hole game and would probably take up only two and a half hours of your time. But if you don't want to go with me, I'll understand."

"Becky, it's entirely unfair of you to pull at my heartstrings on this. I don't know if I can even remember how to hit the ball."

"You don't have to be an expert, Mom. There will be lots of people at a beginner level. It's the participation and support for the cause that are important."

"Oh, okay. Tell me where to be and when."

"That's great, Mom. Thank you. The event is the first weekend of next month, and I'll pick you up. We can discuss what time is best as we get closer to the event."

"What will I need to bring, Bec?"

"I'll have your clubs and tees. All you'll need is an extra pair of pants."

Patty laughed. "Excuse me? Why do I need an extra pair of pants?"

"In case you get a hole in one." Becky hardly got the words out before she started giggling.

Patty looked up and saw that Rick was watching her. She smiled and shook her head before responding to Becky's joke. "Rebecca O'Toole, there is no doubt you are Maggie O'Toole's granddaughter."

"I know, Mom. And I hope I can always make you laugh like she does. Gotta go now. Thanks again for agreeing to join my golf foursome."

"I'm happy to help out, Bec. Love you."

"You, too, Mom."

Rick waited for Patty to end the call and then paused in his writing. "I couldn't help but hear your side of that conversation, and I'm dying to know why you need a second pair of pants to play golf."

Patty gave Rick the punch line and explained the purpose of the game. "Have you ever played golf?"

"No. It was never my interest. I preferred to hike or bike-ride during my free time."

Patty lifted her eyebrows. "Do you still have your bike?"

"I do. I brought it with me when I moved out here from Boston, thinking I'd use it on the trails. Haven't taken it out of my garage other than for my brief move to Salem and back."

Patty smiled. "I have a bike that I haven't used in ten years. Let's go for a bike ride!"

Rick laughed. "Is there something going on that I should know about? First, dinner tomorrow. Now a bike ride?"

Patty looked down at her desk. "I just thought it would be fun. Forget I mentioned it."

Rick was silent as he too looked down at his desk. After a couple of minutes, he spoke up. "I'll get my bike out and make sure it's in riding condition. If it is, I'd like for us to go on a ride. You pick the place and time."

Patty continued to study her report. "Okay." She looked up and smiled at Rick.

CHAPTER FOURTEEN

The next morning, Brad walked into the office. "Your appointments are here. Who do you want first?"

"Connor," said Patty. "We'll be in there in a minute." She stared out the window. "If there's a reason why Connor hasn't become good buddies with Max, what is it and how do we get him to give it up?"

"I've been thinking about the same question," said Rick. "The fact that Max doesn't have a record for assault doesn't mean he hasn't hurt anyone. I think he has. He may have come close to murder before, and he's just not yet been arrested."

"I agree, Rick. Killing Jerry wasn't a spur-of-the-moment or temporary-insanity murder of passion. It was premeditated and calculating. It's hard to comprehend how someone went to the trouble of putting peanut oil on Jerry's mouthpiece to disable him and then, as if that wasn't enough, injecting a fatal dose of a drug that assured the man's death. This killer is smart, and he did his homework prior to committing the murder."

"He's got an evil side to him, Patty. And evil people usually work their way up to killing. They've caused harm to animals and/or people before. We think Max is our murderer, and I think that Connor and Trevor know something about the brutal side of Max that they're not telling us. Let's approach them in that vein."

Patty nodded. "I'll start with a couple of questions, and then you take over. If either of them needs more encouragement, I'll step in again. We just need one major assault episode to get us our warrant."

Connor was seated in a relaxed position when the detectives walked in. Rick sat down, opened his file, and pulled a pencil from his pocket. Patty sat down and faced Connor.

"How are you, Connor? Done any fishing lately?"

Connor leaned his chair back on two legs. "Yeah."

"What did you catch?"

"Mostly rockfish."

"Been back to Diver Rock?"

"No."

"You're aware of why you're here. We want to know more about Max Rainy."

"Yeah, I got that. But I can't tell you any more than I already have. I don't know him very well, and I don't know who killed that missing diver."

"We understand, Connor, that you don't know Max well, and we're not here to talk about the missing diver. But there is something you know about Max that we want you to tell us about."

Connor shrugged. "What's that?"

"Something that Max did to someone else that caused a lot of pain. You know that Max can be brutal. We need to know what he's done and to whom."

Connor fidgeted in his chair, and he exhaled loudly. "I don't know what you're talking about."

Patty sat back. Rick closed his file and leaned forward. "Connor, do you know what an accessory to the crime is?"

"Yeah, I think so."

"Tell me what you think it is," said Rick.

Connor looked down at the table. "It's someone who helps with a crime."

Rick nodded. "That's good, Connor. That's part of the definition. It can also be someone who knows a crime's been committed and remains silent to protect the criminal. Is that what you're doing, Connor? Are you lying to protect Max from some past crime he committed?"

The color began to change on Connor's face. "No. That's not what I'm doing. I don't know who killed that diver."

"I'm not talking about the diver, Connor. But Max hurt someone else. Maybe almost killed him. You know what he did, and you're lying to protect Max. Do you know what happens to people who are convicted of being an accessory to a crime? They go to prison, Connor."

Connor sat wringing his hands and staring at the table.

Rick leaned forward and raised his voice. "Connor! What did Max do to hurt someone? Quit protecting him and tell us what you know!"

Patty sat forward again. "Save yourself, Connor. Save yourself and help us put Max away. What did he do?"

Connor slowly lifted his head and looked at Patty. "If I tell you, and Max finds out, he'll kill me."

"If you don't tell us, we will find out from someone else, and you'll go to prison for protecting him. Now, Connor, what did Max do? Who did he hurt?"

Connor looked at Rick and back at Patty. "He beat a guy up so bad he went to the hospital. I think he lost one of his eyes."

Patty glanced at Rick and proceeded to question Connor. "When was this, Connor?"

"Four or five years ago. I wasn't there, but I heard about it from someone who knew the guy that was beat up."

"What's the victim's name? Where does he live?"

"His name was Tim, I think. I don't remember a last name. I heard he moved out of Brookings when he got out of the hospital."

"Why didn't he file a police report?"

"I heard he was a dealer and knew he'd go to prison if he ratted on Max. Max knew about the drugs."

Patty continued, quickly responding with questions to keep Connor talking. "Do you know where he moved?"

"No. But I know someone who does."

"Who is that?"

"His name's Peter Sham."

"Why do you think Peter Sham knows?"

"Because the guy who Max beat up was Peter's best buddy."

Patty looked at Rick. He nodded and leaned forward. "One last question, Connor. Do you know why Max beat up the guy named Tim?"

"I heard it was because Tim said something bad about Max's sister. I don't know what, but it made Max go ballistic."

"Okay, Connor," Patty said. "Thanks for coming in. We're going to ask Stuart a few questions and then the two of you can go."

Connor stood up nervously. "You won't tell anyone what I told you, will you?"

"Not unless we have to," said Patty.

Connor walked out with Brad. The detectives remained seated.

"Well," said Patty, "now we know why Peter Sham is terrified of Max."

"Yeah, and Peter's got the information we need for our warrant. Let's see if Trevor can tell us anything we don't already know."

The door opened and Brad sent Trevor into the room.

"Hi, Trevor," said Patty. "Thanks for coming in. Connor said you've been doing some fishing lately."

"Yeah. I don't know why you want to talk with me again. I don't know anything about Max except that he fishes."

"Oh," said Patty, "I think you know him better than that."

Trevor slowly sat up in his chair. "What do you mean?"

"We think you know that Max has an evil side to him. That he can be pretty brutal."

"I, I don't know what you mean."

"Sure you do, Trevor. Max once beat a guy so bad that the guy was hospitalized. But then you know about that. Don't you?"

Trevor was looking from Patty to Rick and back. He looked surprised at Patty's comment.

"I don't know," he said.

"You do know, Trevor. And what we want to know is the name of the victim and where he lives."

Rick spoke to Trevor as he did with Connor about being an accessory to the crime.

"You can't put me in prison. I didn't hurt anybody. And I don't know who that guy is that Max attacked. Max hurts people, and he'll hurt me if I talk about him."

Rick slowly spoke to Trevor. "Should we talk to Peter Sham?"

Trevor's face drained of color. "I don't know that guy. I don't know any of Max's friends. Connor and I just keep to ourselves. We don't want no part of Max or Peter. I can't tell you anything."

Patty and Rick gave each other a glance suggesting the interview should end.

Patty turned back to Trevor. "We don't have any more questions. But you need to call us if you think of anything else about the guy Max beat up."

Trevor stood up and quickly walked out the door Brad had opened. The detectives headed down the hall. Rick stopped at the break room, picked up a few cookies, and brought them back to the office. Patty picked up their coffee mugs and got them both a refill.

She set her coffee on the desk. "I guess we know, now, why Max gave Jerry's knife to Peter. Peter knows about the earlier assault."

Rick washed the cookie down with coffee before talking. "Yeah. Peter may be telling the truth about Jerry's death. He may not have been there to see it."

Patty sipped her coffee. "How are we going to get Peter to give us the name and address of the victim? He's terrified of Max, and for good reason."

With another cookie in hand, Rick responded, "Connor said that the incident happened about five years ago. I faintly remember it. We were working on that case where the retired cop was hung in the rest area across from Harris Beach."

Patty looked at Rick. "That's right. I remember Brad and Pete talking about it. The beaten man was brought into Curry General but refused to say who attacked him. The hospital may have a forwarding address."

"I'll check," said Rick. "Do you want to set up another interview with Peter Sham?"

"Yes, but not until you check the hospital for the victim's full name and address. I want to go into the interview already knowing the answers to the questions we'll ask."

"I'll get on it now," said Rick.

"Before you do that," said Patty, "remind me of the timing for your Aunt Mary Lee's arrival. I'm thinking dinner on Saturday would work well if she's coming in on Friday. If not, we can get together on Sunday. I'm just not sure Becky can join us then."

"Saturday should be good. I'll pick her up at the Crescent City airport about seven Friday evening. Saturday, I figured we can visit the stores on Chetco and at the port. I also think she'd enjoy the art galleries. What time do you want us there for dinner?"

Patty thought for a moment. "How about three? That will give us time to visit before dinner. Do you want me to invite Mom and Bill?"

"Sure. That would be good. I'll be pretty much talked out by then, so I'll be grateful for others to keep the conversation going."

Patty smiled. "She'll only be with you a couple of days. Surely you'll find a few things to talk about during that time. Ask her about her life. Do you know what she did for a living and how she spends her time now?"

"Those are good questions, Patty. I'm thinking she was a teacher, but I don't know what grade level or subject. She would have retired about twenty years ago. I'll ask what keeps her busy now."

"Don't worry about what to talk about," Patty said. "It will come to you."

"Okay. What about food? I wonder what she eats for breakfast?"

Patty laughed. "The hotel she's staying at serves breakfast. I imagine she'll eat something there before she meets up with you for the day. You might want to have sandwiches ready on Friday. It will probably be too late to go out to eat once you get her to her hotel and she settles in. Saturday you can ask her what she wants to do for lunch, knowing that you'll eat dinner at my place. Why don't you plan to BBQ on Sunday?"

Rick exhaled and lowered his shoulders. "You make it sound easy."

"It will be. Let me know if you want help with the BBQ. I could bring a salad and a side dish."

Rick smiled. "That would be great. I'll get the steaks. She'll have to be at the airport Monday morning at six-thirty. Maybe I can buy a couple of pastries on Sunday for us to have with coffee before we leave for the airport."

"I think she'd like that, Rick. I'm sure she's going to enjoy the time she gets to spend with you. I'm looking forward to meeting her."

"Great," said Rick. "Now that we've planned for her visit, I'll see what I can find out about Max's beating victim being admitted to Curry General. I'm guessing this shouldn't take long."

"After you talk with the hospital, I'll contact Peter Sham. I'm hoping that Peter's name may be included in the Curry General information."

"You mean like maybe it was Peter who admitted the victim?"

"Precisely," said Patty. "That would give us what we need to link the two together and get us closer to a search warrant for Max's house. I'll write up a report on this morning's interviews while you talk with Curry General."

Forty minutes later, Patty looked up at Rick when he ended the call. "What I could hear sounded promising. Did you get what we need?"

Rick finished writing on his notepad. "I did. The victim's name was Timothy Rollins. He was brought into the hospital by a friend, Peter Sham. The last address they have for Rollins is in Cave Junction."

"Well, that's interesting," said Patty. "I wonder if one or both of the Stengle brothers knew Rollins? We need to talk with Randy again. But let's talk with Peter first, now that we know the connection between him and Timothy Rollins. I'll ask Brad to set up the interview. Did the hospital give you a phone number for Rollins?"

"They did. I'll try it, but after five years he may have moved out of the area."

"If it doesn't work, look for the Rollins name in Cave Junction. He may have family there even if he's moved away."

Patty walked down the hall and spoke with Brad. She returned to her office and walked to the window. "It's a beautiful day out there," she said out loud to Rick. "Sixty-six degrees and no wind. The weather doesn't get much better than this. Brad will set up an interview for us at the jail with Peter Sham. Did you find anything on Rollins?"

"First, the weather is great, and I'm glad we have an office window for you to look out of. And, yes, I spoke with his parents. They said Tim moved away out of fear, and they're not sure where he now lives. His mom will contact a few people who might know and get back with me. She and Tim's father would like to see Max hang for what he did to their son. Something else. Tim went to Illinois Valley High School. The same school Max and Jerry attended. Tim's mother said that Max had a temper even then and went off the rails after his sister was killed."

"That's good information, Rick. We're learning more about Max with every person we talk to. I'd like to set up an appointment with Tim's parents to learn more about Max's relationship with their son. They may be able to tell us more about Jerry too."

Brad stepped through the office door. "You've got an appointment with Peter Sham tomorrow at nine. The jailer's expecting you."

Patty made note in her phone. "Thanks, Brad." She stood up and put her jacket on. "I'm going home now to get ready for our dinner tonight. How about I meet you at the restaurant at six?"

Rick glanced at his watch. "I wasn't planning on dressing up. Is what I've got on okay with you?"

Patty smiled. "It's fine. I'll see you in a couple of hours."

Rick picked up his pen and continue working on his report.

* * *

The restaurant was busy, and Rick hadn't thought to make a reservation. "Looks like we'll have a twenty- to thirty-minute wait. Is that okay with you or do you want to try someplace else?"

"The wait is fine. We could have something to drink while we're waiting."

"Okay. I'll get it. What would you like?"

"I'd like a glass of cabernet."

Rick nodded and turned toward the bar. "I'll be right back. Why don't you find us a couple of seats in the lounge so that we can enjoy our drinks and an hors d'oeuvre."

Patty found them seats at a small table. Rick set the drinks down.

"A cab for you and a Coke for me. I also brought us each a menu so that we have time to make a decision before we get a table."

Patty picked up her glass of wine. "To good friends," she toasted. Rick picked up his Coke and they gently bumped glasses. Rick and Patty locked eyes and neither of them spoke. A crimson color began to slowly climb up Patty's neck. She quickly looked down at the menu. "I already know what I want," she said.

Rick sipped his Coke. "That was fast. What are you thinking will be good?"

"I think it's all probably good, but I'm having a steak and potato."

"That sounds great to me too, Patty. I'll have the same. How about I order a plate of calamari to tide us over until dinner is served?"

"I love calamari!"

CHAPTER FIFTEEN

Peter Sham sat quietly waiting in the interview room. He sat leaning back on the legs of his chair, looking quite sure of himself except for rubbing his hands back and forth on his knees.

The detectives sat down. Rick was prepared with pencil and pad to take notes.

"Peter Sham," Patty said, "thanks for agreeing to see us."

"No problem," said Peter, staring down at his hands. "I don't understand why you're here again since there's nothing I can tell you about Max or Jerry's death."

"We appreciate that there's little you know about Jerry's death. We believed you when you told us that you were not there when Jerry was killed. We have, however, learned something new that may help in your understanding of why we're here." Patty stared at the young man, giving him no indication of there being any mistake in what she was about to say.

"New information?"

Patty kept her voice calm and her gaze spot on. "We now know, Peter, about Timothy Rollins. We know it was you who admitted Timothy to Curry General. This new information brings up additional questions for you."

Peter brought his chair upright and sank into it as though his body could meld into the frame. He no longer rubbed his knees but rather held his hands in a tight grip on top of the table.

Patty continued. "What we don't get is how you could turn your back on such a good friend. He nearly died. He lost the sight of one eye. That will affect his employment opportunities for the rest of his life. You cared enough to drop him off at the hospital, but not enough to turn in the guy who nearly killed him?"

Patty paused and Rick leaned forward to speak. "Or maybe that wasn't care you were feeling for your friend. Maybe you were just trying to get rid of the evidence that would convict Max. Maybe you'd have been just as happy dropping Tim off in a dumpster."

Peter turned beet red as he brought his hands up on top of the table. He leaned forward toward Rick as he began to physically shake. "I would not have dropped him off in a dumpster." Tears began to well up in Peter's eyes and drain into the creases between his nose and cheeks. "Tim was the only real friend I've ever known. When my mom left and my dad became a drunk, it was Tim who sat with me during school lunch hour. When the other kids would all go home at the end of the day, it was Tim who rode his bike with me to the park and talked about life, his and mine. I could tell him what it was like at home since my mom died, and he'd assure me life would get better once I had a high school diploma and could earn my own way."

Patty glanced at Rick before addressing Peter. She sat forward and spoke softly. "Then why, Peter? Why agree with Max to say nothing about Tim's beating? Why say nothing to us when you know that Max put your best friend in the hospital?"

Tears now streamed down Peter's face, and he choked on his words. "Look at me. Do I look like someone who has the courage to stand up to Max? Do I look like someone who has the courage to go to court on behalf of my best friend?"

Patty and Rick sat quietly, waiting for Peter to continue.

"I was beaten by my dad almost every day after my mother died. From the age of thirteen to not long ago. I lived in fear and pain. No one could help me. I saw Max beat Tim and I did nothing. Then, before Max left, he walked up to me. He knew Tim was my best friend. He told me that he'd do the same to me if I told anyone what happened. He expected Tim to die and so did I."

Patty slowly exhaled as she realized the pain this young man carried.

As he finished, Peter looked directly into Patty's eyes. "I am a worthless person. I know that. And if I had any courage at all, I'd have turned Max in for beating Tim. But I'm not a hero, Detective O'Toole. I'm a coward." Peter glanced back and forth between Patty and Rick before completing his thought. "I am ashamed of the coward within me, but I'm terrified to think of what Max will do to me if I speak up against him. I'll kill myself before I let him beat me the way he beat Tim."

Patty and Rick sat looking at a man who had nothing left to tell. Patty glanced at Rick, and he broke the silence. "Okay, Peter. I understand why you fear Max Rainy. But I don't believe that you'll ever be able to forgive yourself for abandoning your friend."

"Unless," Patty interrupted, "you stand up for your best friend. You do something courageous for both of you. You help us to bring Max Rainy to his knees in court. You testify if we bring him in."

Peter was motionless as he looked at Patty. "I can't."

"But you can, Peter. You can help us put Max away for the rest of his life. You can live in peace, knowing that you vindicated yourself in honor of your best friend. Agree to testify, Peter. Your testimony will allow us to search Max's home, and we believe that search will uncover evidence relating to the death of Jerry Stengle. You'll never have to fear Max again."

The room was like a dark cave hidden deep underground. Total silence. Not even the sound of breathing. Then Peter's voice, small and quiet. "I won't tell you anything more. I won't testify against Max."

The detectives glanced at each other. Rick closed his file.

"Thanks for answering our questions, Peter," said Patty. The door opened and a deputy stood waiting to escort Peter back to his cell. Rick and Patty drove back to their office.

After returning to their desks, Patty sat down and loudly exhaled. "That was pathetic. And I am now convinced that we must put Max away for a long, long time."

Rick put his jacket around the back of his chair. "Yeah. It was. I think we should use Peter's confession to get a warrant to search Max's house."

Patty nodded. "I agree. We may not need a hearing. I'll write up the affidavit and get it to the judge."

CHAPTER SIXTEEN

Patty rode her bike up next to Rick at Bankus Park, where they'd agreed to meet. "So where do you want to ride?"

Rick shrugged. "The bike ride is your idea. I'll ride anywhere you want to go."

Patty turned her bike toward the crosswalk. "Okay. Let's cross here and ride north to Harris Beach State Park. We can stop in the parking area and watch the ocean for a while before riding on to Dawson Street, where we'll turn around. Then we'll ride south to Arnold and wind our way to Railroad. We can ride along Railroad back to Chetco, cross the bridge, and ride down to the port." Patty smiled. "Any questions?"

"None at the moment. I believe I followed that without a problem. Do we need to pick up some food, like a snack or something, before we take off?"

Patty laughed. "It won't take us that long to get to the port. I've got water and a healthy snack bar for each of us. We'll eat lunch at the port. Is that going to be okay with you?"

"Sure. But I'd like to carry my snack bar."

Ten minutes later they were at Harris Beach State Park watching the ocean.

Rick got off his bike, put the kickstand down, and walked up to the edge of the parking lot. "What a spectacular view. It's days like this that remind me why I live here."

"I love it too, Rick. We are fortunate to be able to live and work in such a beautiful area of the country." Patty pointed off to the left. "Look. An osprey with a fish in its talons."

Rick caught sight of the bird. "He appears to be looking for a safe place to land and enjoy the lunch he caught. Those seagulls flying around him are thinking otherwise. I've seen a lot of ospreys out here. Do you know if they're found only along the coast?"

"I do know. I helped Becky with research for a report on the osprey when she was in high school. Ospreys are found along coastlines, lakes, and rivers almost worldwide. They are sometimes called a sea hawk, river hawk, or fish hawk. They're diurnal, meaning that they're active during the day and rest at night. Anything else you'd like to know about the bird?"

"You do know your ospreys. How big are they relative to, say, an eagle?"

"No contest there. The bald eagle is one of the largest birds in North America. The osprey has a fifty-nine- to seventy-inch wingspan and weighs three to four pounds. The bald eagle has an eighty-inch wingspan and weighs six and a half to almost fourteen pounds!"

Rick raised his eyebrows. "Seems the bald eagle could eat the osprey for lunch if he wanted."

Patty laughed. "It could. Speaking of lunch, ready to continue our adventure?"

Rick walked back to his bike. "This was a good idea, Patty. I'm enjoying our ride already."

Patty led off on her bike. "Tell me that again this afternoon after we've been on our bikes for a few more hours."

* * *

The next morning Patty arrived at the office with a smile. "Good morning. Any soreness in the legs after our ride?"

"None at all, surprisingly. I enjoyed that."

Patty hung her jacket over the back of her chair. "The bike ride or spending the afternoon with me?"

Rick paused before speaking and looked at Patty. "Well, both I guess."

Patty nodded silently.

"Is that okay?" he asked.

"More than," Patty replied.

Rick smiled slightly and opened a file.

"Has your aunt called to confirm you'll be there this evening?"

"No. She knows I'll be there to pick her up. I plan to leave Brookings this evening at six to cover any delays due to roadwork. There has been a traffic light just beyond the main exit for Smith River, directing one-way traffic and causing a five-minute delay. I don't know if the work has been completed."

Patty opened the file on her desk. "Five minutes wouldn't be a bad wait. Did you see the digital sign for motorists traveling south on Highway 101? It warns travelers to expect up to a two-hour delay at Last Chance Grade."

"I did see that," said Rick. "I'm glad we have no need to travel south of Crescent City."

"Knock on wood," said Patty. "What a nightmare for people who live in Klamath and work in Crescent City or further north. I expect there are some days when they just must let their employers know they can't get to work. So, about your aunt. I'm looking forward to meeting her."

"Yeah, I'm looking forward to meeting her again. I have so little family. No appointments today so I'm planning to finish my reports. That should make the LT happy."

* * *

Patty answered her front door to welcome Rick and his aunt Mary Lee.

"Welcome," she said. "Come in."

Mary Lee stepped in, and Rick introduced her to Patty. Becky, Maggie, and Bill came out of the kitchen to say hi to Rick and meet his aunt.

Patty stepped back to let Becky greet the new visitor. "Becky," Patty said, "this is Mary Lee. Mary Lee, this is my daughter Becky." They shook hands.

Becky looked up at Rick. "Hey, Rick."

"Hey, Becky. How's the studying going?"

"It's going," said Becky.

Patty then introduced her mother and Bill. "This is my mother, Maggie, and her husband, Bill."

Maggie extended her hand. "It's so nice to meet you, Mary Lee. We are all very fond of Rick, and it's great to meet a member of his family."

Mary Lee smiled. "Rick told me a little about you while driving from the airport to my hotel. He's clearly very fond of you too."

Bill extended his hand. "A pleasure to meet you, Mary Lee."

Mary Lee smiled. "Ah, yes. The gambler."

Everyone laughed as Bill enjoyed the reference with pride. "Not so much anymore but certainly for enough years to earn the handle."

"Oh? Does that mean you are no longer taking part in the game?"

Bill smiled. "*Gotta know when to fold 'em.* Nowadays I spend my time with Maggie, Oscar, and friends."

Mary Lee looked around. "Oscar?"

Maggie smiled. "Oscar is not sharing this evening with us. He's our young dachshund."

Rick offered to get drinks while Maggie and Patty went into the kitchen for the hors d'oeuvres. Once out of hearing range from Bill, Maggie asked Patty, "Notice anything different about Bill?"

"Well, it's funny you should ask, Mom. I cringed when Mary Lee asked him a question, worried he wouldn't hear a word. But he understood perfectly." Patty saw her mother smile broadly. "Did he get hearing aids?"

"He did! And it's like the world has opened up for him. He hears sounds he hasn't heard for years. Like the waves lapping at the shore, or the singing birds in the tree beside our deck. I can talk to him from across the room, and he hears and understands every word I say. And his responses make sense!"

"I'm happy for you, Mom, and for Bill. I know that the two of you have had a difficult time conversing."

Maggie shook her head. "Difficult? You know how people talk out loud and when questioned about it say that they're just talking to themselves? Well, I've been talking to myself for three years."

Patty laughed. "Oh, Mom. You could do stand-up with that line. It couldn't have been that bad."

Maggie laughed too. "Pretty close. Anyway, having him hear again is great for both of us. And wait until you hear him talk about his hearing aids. He can operate them from his phone!"

"From his phone? I will have to ask him about it. Maybe not this evening, though. I don't want to embarrass him."

"Embarrass Bill? You won't, Patty. And I know he'd love to explain how they work."

"Okay, I'll ask if an appropriate moment comes up. Will you take in these hors d'oeuvre plates and napkins for everyone? You can then join in on the conversation out there and ask Becky to come in and help me."

"Will do. Oh, here she comes now."

"Hi, Mom. Can I help?"

"Thanks, Bec. If you'll take the tray in and let each person choose what they want from it, I'll help Rick with the drinks."

Becky picked up the tray. "I'll serve these and then come back in to help with anything else."

"Great, Bec."

Maggie distributed the plates and napkins and sat down next to Bill and across from Mary Lee. "Did you enjoy a comfortable flight out here?"

"It was uneventful, which, for me, is comfortable. I was pleasantly surprised at how nice the Crescent City airport is. I expected something more like a small, windowless building."

Maggie raised her eyebrows. "The Del Norte County Regional Airport is new, but your description is not far off from what the old airport looked like. Bill and I use it a lot since it now provides daily flights to and from Oakland."

Becky walked around the room with the serving tray. "Would you like some cheese and crackers or a spring roll?" she asked, lowering the tray for Mary Lee.

Mary Lee picked up the small tongs utensil and lifted some of each on to her plate. "This looks lovely."

Becky served the others and then returned to the kitchen to help her mom.

Patty checked the meat in the oven and took off her apron. "Let's go enjoy the conversation, Bec. You can help me serve dinner when it's time."

Patty took a seat near Rick's aunt. "Tell us a little about yourself, Mary Lee. Rick seemed to recall that you were a teacher."

Mary Lee looked warmly at Rick. "I'm pleased he remembered. He's only met me a couple of time before this evening, and that was years ago. I taught school for thirty years."

"What grade level?" Becky asked.

"Several grade levels, all between third and eighth. I taught in two different parochial schools for most of my career."

Patty noticed Becky paying close attention to Mary Lee and wanted the conversation on teaching to continue. "Why did you choose to teach in parochial schools?"

"That's a good question, Patty. The parochial schools' administrations were able to require discipline. This meant children were expected to arrive in their classrooms on time, remain quiet in the classroom except when asked to speak, and complete their daily homework. They wore uniforms. That eliminated the fashion shows that take place in many public schools, where some girls wear the shortest and tightest clothes they can get away with. The rules and clothing standards provided fewer distractions from the real reason the students were there, which was to learn.

"I mentioned teaching in parochial schools for most of my career. My first four years of teaching were in a public school. In the nineteen-sixties and seventies, there were several changes within the public school system, and many teachers lost their ability to require order in the classroom. Without being able to discipline students, the rowdy students often took over the class. The breakdown extended to junior colleges, many of which changed their grading system to a pass/fail system, allowing students to obtain a degree without ever earning at least an average grade.

"Another problem was with the design of the schools themselves. Some were built with open doorways, and dividing walls that rose only part of the way up toward the ceiling. This resulted in an infiltration of noise into every classroom, making it near impossible for a teacher to maintain the attention of her or his students. I felt sorry for the students amid all of this because they were the real losers. They did not receive the education they needed to make their way in life.

"Oh, my, I'm doing all the talking. You can see that teaching and the need to learn are subjects about which I have strong opinions."

"I'm finding your experience very interesting," said Becky. "Please go on."

Mary Lee looked at the others, all of whom nodded in agreement. "When I interviewed at the first parochial school in which I taught, I asked specifically about what behaviors in children were or were not tolerated. It was explained to me like this: Parents send their children to school to learn. If a child misbehaves, we give the parent an ultimatum. Either the child follows the rules or is taken out of the school. You'd be surprised how well-mannered children can be in a learning environment when parents stand behind the rules and teachers.

"Oh, there were a few bad teachers over the years, like there are bad apples in every profession. They were dismissed from the parochial schools. That's another big difference between public and private schools. Public school teachers have tenure within a few years of teaching. This makes it near impossible to remove a poor teacher from the teaching profession. The result is that teachers who are inadequate, usually because they don't have their heart in teaching, continue to hold children hostage in their toxic classroom environment. This is an unfortunate fact that dilutes the reputation of good public school teachers. Although I've used parochial schools as a private school example, the charter schools with which I'm familiar also have good reputations."

Becky was sitting on the edge of her chair. "You sound like you were a great teacher."

Mary Lee smiled. "Thank you, Becky. I deeply loved teaching and turned out many wonderful students. Some of them continue to stay in touch and keep me up on their lives. Now, Miss Becky, enough about me. Tell me what you're studying."

Becky talked about her current studies and desire to work with large animals. "I never thought of teaching, but after listening to you, I think I'd enjoy it once I have my degree. You've inspired me!"

Mary Lee smiled. "That makes me happy. Maybe you'll write now and then and, like my students, keep me abreast of what you do in life."

"Oh, I'd like that very much. Thank you. I'll definitely be writing."

The conversation paused, and Bill looked around the room. "I'd like to let those of you who know me know that I've heard every word of Mary Lee's communication about her career. I've heard her through the help of my new high-tech hearing aids."

Rick looked at Bill. "You're wearing hearing aids? I don't see them."

"They're in my ears. Unlike hearing aids people wore a few decades ago, these are tiny and exceptionally light. I hardly feel them."

Maggie gave Patty an "I told you" smile. Mary Lee leaned forward trying to find the hearing aid in Bill's ears. "Does the soft music in the background affect your ability to hear our conversation?"

"Not at all. My hearing aids are programmed to eliminate the surrounding noise and zero in on just the conversation I want to hear. They are also paired to my phone. I can widen or narrow the sound path using an app on my phone. I can also answer my cell phone by merely tapping twice on my ear. They make watching TV a much better experience because I can listen to the TV directly through my hearing aids. Therefore, if Maggie is watching with me, the volume doesn't need to be increased for my benefit."

"That's pretty amazing," said Mary Lee. "I've recently had my hearing checked, and hearing aids were recommended. I looked no further into it because I can remember my late husband's difficult experience with them. It seems they've come a long way since then."

Bill agreed. "Yes, they have. I didn't realize how much I was missing until I began wearing them. And I'm sorry for Maggie's sake that it took me so long to get my hearing checked."

Maggie smiled. "Well, I'm just glad they've worked out so well. It's a blessing to be able to again hold a conversation without needing to raise my voice."

Patty stood up. "On that note, dinner is served. Everyone please come to the table and sit wherever you'd like. Becky, will you please help me put dinner on the table?"

CHAPTER SEVENTEEN

Rick walked into the office with a small white bakery bag. "Help yourself, if interested."

"I was hoping you'd have pastries. I left the house this morning without eating. Did Mary Lee get off okay?"

"She did. She told me I have wonderful friends and that she hopes to see us again if we're ever out her way."

"I enjoyed meeting her too, and I know everyone was interested in her academic career. She may have inspired Becky toward teaching."

Rick nodded. "Yeah. I saw how Bec seemed mesmerized by my aunt's stories."

Patty smiled. "That's the first time I've heard you call Becky 'Bec.'"

"It is? I guess it might be the first time. It seems kind of natural since I hear you call her Bec all the time."

"I think she'd like it, Rick."

Patty's phone chimed. "O'Toole. Before you go any further, Chief, let me put you on speaker phone so that my partner can hear." Patty put the phone on speaker and let Rick know who was calling. "It's Chief Petty Officer Walker of the Coast Guard about our three guys who took their boat up the coast."

"Good morning, Chief Petty Officer. This is Detective Rick Starker."

"Hello, Detective. I called this morning to let you both know that your instincts were accurate. We boarded the boat you described and found drugs with enough street value to buy another three boats. We also confiscated their list of buyers. There's a couple of Curry County names on here that will be of interest to the two of you."

"Congratulations on the bust, Chief," said Patty. "We'll follow up on those names. It's good to know they won't be bringing their drugs to Brookings again."

"We wouldn't have known to stop them if not for your hunch, Detective O'Toole."

"Yeah," said Rick. "She gets those a lot, and they've helped us solve more than one big case."

Patty rolled her eyes at Rick. "Let us know if you need one of us to testify when this goes to trial."

"I'll do that. You two stay safe."

"Thanks, Chief," said Patty. She ended the call. "That's rewarding. Another supplier off the street."

"Yep. I'm guessing we may recognize the names of the dealers."

Patty's email pinged. "He's just sent them. I'll give these to Brad and ask him to get the addresses for us. We need to make this a priority before they get wind that something's up and flee."

Patty walked down the hall to talk with Brad. "Check with PO Heart and find out if these guys are already in the system. It might be easier to find them."

"I'll do it now," said Brad.

Before sitting back down at her desk, Patty reached for her coffee cup and offered to pick up Rick's too. "Brad's checking with Heart. I'm going for a refill. Want one?"

Rick held out his cup. "Thanks."

Brad was walking into the detectives' office as Patty returned with the coffees. "PO Heart knows both of them," he said. "I've got addresses."

Patty looked up at Rick. "We'll need enough backup to cover the front, back, and both ends of the street. I'll let the LT know and complete an affidavit for a search warrant for each house. I'll also call the Sheriff since one of these is a Harbor address." She walked down the hall to the lieutenant's office. The blind on his interior office window was open, allowing Patty to be seen as she approached his door. The other window looked out on the street.

"Come in, O'Toole." Patty had never known the lieutenant to use anything but last names. Recent photos of his wife and children sat on his desk. On the wall behind his desk hung three plaques thanking him for his volunteer service with local Little League teams. Also on the wall was a "Coach of the Year" award from Special Olympics. The lieutenant waited for Patty to sit down. "Have you received the warrant you requested for Max Rainy's house?"

"Not yet, LT. But I was told the judge had been gone a couple of days on emergency leave so, if it's approved, I expect we'll get it today or tomorrow. I'm here to let you know the status on another matter."

The lieutenant sat back in his chair. "I'm listening."

"You remember the three guys who docked at the port on their way up the coast?"

"I do. You called the Coast Guard. Did they find reason to board the boat?"

"They did, LT. And they found a large haul of drugs. The Coasties also found a list of dealers including two in Curry County who made purchases while the boat was docked here. We've got names and addresses. One lives in Brookings. The other in Harbor. I'd like to get search warrants and call the Sheriff and OSP to coordinate a bust as soon as possible. I may need four of our officers, in addition to Rick and me. We can use the Sheriff's reserves for traffic and transportation of the suspects. Do I have your approval?"

"You do. I suggest you move quickly. Word will travel fast."

Patty stood to leave. "Thanks, LT." As she turned to exit, the lieutenant spoke.

"Detective O'Toole."

Patty stopped and turned around. "LT?"

"These guys are going to be armed, and they'll know, when they're surrounded, that they're out of options. This situation will require that you move quickly. Just be sure to make every action deliberate. No guessing. You may have to use your firearms. There's no doubt we want these guys, but safety comes first."

"Understood, LT." Patty walked back to her office and shared the information with Rick and Brad. "I'll complete the affidavit then call the Sheriff while the two of you identify another three officers. My hope is that we can be ready in two days."

Patty gave the completed affidavit to Brad then picked up her phone and hit speed-dial. The Sheriff answered after three rings. "Hello, Sheriff, this is Detective O'Toole."

"Good morning, Detective. You must need my help."

Patty smiled. "We do." She explained the situation. "Would you have three or four deputies who can assist with the Harbor residence and a few reserves who can help where needed?"

The Sheriff paused. "I've got to keep some of my deputies in the central and north county, but I can give you two for sure. I might have a third, but I suggest you find out how many troopers OSP can send."

"Thanks, Sheriff. I appreciate the help. I will be calling the state police. Can we set up a task force meeting for tomorrow at three here at my department? I'm thinking we can plan our strategy tomorrow and carry it out early the following day."

"That will work. I'll have my deputies there."

Rick was on his phone when Patty ended her call. She checked her phone contacts and put in the number for Sergeant Jeremy Steadman.

"Detective Patty O'Toole. To what do I owe this honor?"

"Hey, Jeremy. How are things on our highways?"

"Keeping me busy, Patty. What's up?"

"We've learned of two drug dealers living and distributing here in Curry County. One each in Brookings and Harbor. We want to do a bust at both addresses simultaneously. I'm setting up a task force meeting tomorrow afternoon at three with plans to carry out the bust the following day. We need help."

"How much help are you in need of?"

"Three or four troopers."

"Three or four? That's a lot. I doubt we can loan you that many and still maintain a presence where it's needed. I can probably get you one and possibly two. Let me work on it, and I'll get back to you in a while."

"Thanks, Jeremy. Anyone you can spare will be appreciated."

Patty ended the call and filled Rick in on her conversation.

"We should be fine," Rick said. "Even if we get only two each from OSP and the Sheriff, we'll have a law enforcement presence of ten. We can manage with five at each house."

Brad walked into the office and handed Patty an envelope. "You've got your search warrant for Rainy's house."

Patty smiled. "Great! Thanks, Brad." She pulled the warrant out of the envelope and showed it to Rick. "We now have one warrant and hope to have a second by tomorrow's meeting."

"When it rains…" said Rick.

Patty started out the door. "I'll talk with the LT. Maybe we can do the search this afternoon. It shouldn't take more than a couple of hours. Brad and Pete can help us out."

Patty met with the LT and explained. "We've got the search warrant for Max Rainy's house. Rick and I would like to move on it this afternoon. Brad and Pete can assist. Is this okay with you?"

The lieutenant nodded. "Go," he said, "and be careful."

Patty, Rick, Brad, and Pete drove to Max's house. Brad and Pete walked around to watch the back of the house while Rick and Patty approached the front door. Rick knocked, waited thirty seconds, and knocked again.

When the door opened, it was Stuart standing in the doorway. "Max isn't here," he said.

Rick pushed on the door. He and Patty walked in.

"We're not here to see Max," said Patty. "We have a search warrant, and we're here to search the house."

Rick called Brad and let him know to come in. "The front door's unlocked."

"Max isn't going to like this," said Stuart. "I think you should wait for him to get home before you start going through his stuff."

"We're not waiting for Max," said Patty. She searched the couch for any hidden weapons. "I need you to sit down while we're here."

Brad, and Pete Chekowski walked through the front door. Patty nodded toward Pete as she spoke to Stuart. "Officer Chekowski is going to stay and search this room while you wait."

"What are you looking for?" asked Stuart. He stood up from the couch. "You can't keep me here. I'm not under arrest."

Patty ignored his question. "You can leave through the front door."

Stuart got up and walked to the door. "I'm going to call Max. He isn't going to like this at all."

Patty and Rick walked into the garage. There were several boxes on the shelves and a few smaller plastic containers on a tool bench. The detectives began opening them one at a time. Thirty minutes passed as they completed the search of the area.

Patty took in a deep breath and exhaled. "This is disappointing. Not even a syringe. It seemed the logical place for him to keep the drug."

Rick pushed a box back up against the wall. "It does. Maybe Brad or Pete have found something inside."

Brad was in the kitchen. "The refrigerator's pretty much empty other than beer and a few condiments. The freezer's a different story, though it won't be helpful for this search."

Patty looked hopeful. "What did you find?"

"In addition to a few hamburgers, there are four vacuum-packed abalone."

Rick looked at Patty. "Didn't Randy say that Jerry was going abalone-diving with Max?"

Patty looked up at Rick. "He did. Let's take photos. We can't confiscate the mollusks with this warrant, but we can use the photos when questioning Max and Stuart again."

Pete closed a cupboard door. "Nothing. I've also checked the oven, microwave, and hall bathroom. Everything's clean."

"We still have the bedrooms," said Patty. She looked at Brad and Pete. "You two take the right side of the hall, and Rick and I will search the room on the left."

Rick began a search of the closet while Patty went through the desk. The bedroom was compact, with a twin bed, bedside table, lamp, desk, and chair. Patty paused at the desk. "This desk has a docking station for a laptop but no computer. Why would he remove his computer while in town?"

"Good question," said Rick. "I've got nothing in the closet. Ready to move the top mattress?"

Before Patty could answer, they heard someone enter the front door yelling, "What's going on? What are you doing to my house?"

Rick and Patty walked into the living room. Patty pointed toward the kitchen. "The search warrant is on the counter."

Max walked into the kitchen and read the warrant. "Succinylcholine, peanut oil, syringes? What's this about? Why would I have these things?"

"Calm down, Max. We're about done, and I have a question. You have a computer docking station at your desk. Where's your computer?"

Max paced between the living room and kitchen. "I got rid of it." He picked up the warrant and waved it at Patty. "Now, since I know you didn't find any of this stuff in my house, I need you to leave."

Patty looked at Rick. "We've got one last thing to check in your bedroom. Then we'll be on our way."

The detectives lifted the bed mattress and found nothing.

Walking back into the living room, Rick approached Max. "You're hiding something, Max, and we'll eventually find it."

"I haven't done anything," said Max. "And you're not going to find anything that says I have."

The detectives, Brad, and Pete left the house to return to their offices.

"I was so sure we'd find the drug or paraphernalia that would incriminate him," Patty said as they drove off.

"We're missing something," said Rick. "He's guilty. We need to look over our interview notes."

"I don't know how we could have missed something important, but I agree. Let's go over the notes together and brainstorm. But not this afternoon. Let's first take care of tomorrow's bust."

CHAPTER EIGHTEEN

Patty walked into the Emergency Operations Center for the three o'clock meeting. The EOC was divided into several offices and a large meeting room. Seated in the meeting room were two deputies, two troopers, and four police officers. They had a total of ten law enforcement officers including Rick and Patty. Patty stepped up front while Brad and Pete distributed copies of the plan to each task force attendee.

"Good afternoon. Thank you all for being here. We have two individuals, one each in Harbor and Brookings, and each of whom is known to have purchased a large supply of drugs with the intent to sell to members of our community. They purchased the drugs from three guys who traveled by boat from Oakland, CA. The distributors stopped at several ports, including Brookings Harbor, for the sole purpose of selling their load of drugs to dealers at each port.

"We have names and addresses. We're separating into two teams, one for each target. Officer Bradley has distributed a file to each of you. It includes identification of the team you're on. It also includes maps and photos of the target houses and their surrounding neighborhoods. Reserve deputies will keep the area clear of auto and pedestrian traffic during our bust. They will also transport the offenders to the jail. Any questions thus far?" The room remained silent, so Patty continued.

"I will be lead for the Brookings location, and Detective Starker for the house in Harbor. In a few minutes, I will ask that we separate into our teams. The plan is for both teams to simultaneously enter the targeted homes tomorrow morning at six-thirty. It will be light and early enough to hopefully catch the occupants off guard. Are there any questions?"

One of the troopers spoke up. "What about breakfast?"

Patty smiled. "I'm sure your question is appreciated by all. We'll have coffee and pastries here at four-thirty when you arrive. Any other questions? Since I hear none, let's break up into our teams."

Two hours later, Patty and Rick left the EOC and returned to the station. They started down the hall to their office just as the lieutenant was leaving his. They all stopped to talk.

"Detectives. Your search warrants came through."

"That's good news," said Rick.

"How was your meeting?"

"It went well, LT," said Patty. "Brad is coordinating the reserve deputies so that we'll have three at each site. The officers put in place yesterday to watch the targets have confirmed people are going in and out of each house. I hope we can nail the ringleaders."

The LT looked at Rick. "You know to call it off if anything seems other than what you've planned for."

"We know, LT. It should go as planned."

"Good. Give me a status as soon as you can when you've got everything under control."

Patty nodded. "Copy that, LT."

The lieutenant walked down the hall, and Patty and Rick went to their office. They sat down at their desks and began scrolling down emails.

Rick looked up at Patty. "I don't see anything that needs immediate attention. It's after five. Are you interested in an early dinner?"

Patty looked up and smiled. "An early dinner sounds great. I just need to send a quick response to an email."

* * *

The next morning, Patty and Rick arrived at the EOC at four-thirty. Other members of the task force trickled in over the next thirty minutes. The detectives each met with members of their teams, reviewing the plan they'd discussed the prior afternoon. At six-fifteen everyone was ready, and at six twenty-five all task force members left the EOC for their assigned targets.

Patty and one of the deputies pulled up in front of the Brookings house. It was a typical one-story for the neighborhood. The yard was badly overgrown, and the house needed paint. The surveillance officer had reported no sighting of a dog. A second car pulled up, blocking the driveway. An officer and a trooper got out and walked the planned approach to the back of the house. Parked diagonally across the street was a third car. An officer got out and walked to the corner of the house where he could, without moving, watch two sides of the house.

The deputy with Patty carried a ram. Patty knocked loudly on the front door.

"Police. Open up. We have a search warrant." From the corner of her eye, she noticed movement of the curtain in the front window and then heard hollering inside. She stepped away from the doorway and used her radio to let those watching the back of the house know that they were going in.

"Go! Go! Go!"

The deputy hit the door with the ram, breaking it open. A man in the living room ran for the back door while two more came out of the hallway. One brandished a pistol and the other a baseball bat. The man running out the back quickly surrendered to the officer and the trooper entering through the back door.

Patty yelled to the two men who had appeared from the hallway. "Drop your weapons!"

Both men looked back and forth, clearly seeing that they were surrounded. The man with the gun dropped it. There was a wild look in the face of the man with the bat. He started yelling, swung the bat behind him, and charged Patty. The deputy fired and the man went down. He lay on the floor, groaning, as Patty turned him on his stomach, pulled his hands behind his back, and cuffed him. She then nodded to the deputy to follow her down the hall.

Patty checked out one bedroom while the deputy entered the other. "Clear!" Patty yelled.

She then heard a shot in the second bedroom and quickly approached the entrance. A man lay on the floor. A large knife was on the floor about a foot away from the man's hand. He was on his stomach, groaning as blood flowed from his side. The deputy kicked the knife further away from the man and cuffed him.

Patty checked the bathroom at the end of the hall and yelled, "Clear!" She then returned to the deputy. "I'll call for a couple of ambulances. The guy in the living room has meth mouth and all the symptoms of being high now."

Both Patty and the deputy walked back into the living room with the other members of their team. The guy on the floor was rolling back and forth and talking to himself.

"I've called an ambulance for each of these guys. Take the two who are still on their feet out front. Have a couple of reserve deputies take them north to Gold Beach. Notify the LT and the Sheriff so they can get the officer-involved shooting protocol going."

Patty heard sirens and knew the ambulances were minutes away. "Deputy Stanbeck and I will wait for the ambulances to get here. I'll ask for reserves to secure the house. The rest of you can head back to the EOC."

When Patty got into the car to leave, she called Rick on her cell phone. "We're done here. What's your status?"

"We've got four in cuffs. All appear to be strung out, including our dealer. Reserves have taken them up north. How about you?"

"We've got two shot. Neither fatal. They were just taken to Curry General. Three were taken up north. Ask the reserves to secure the house, and you and your team return to the EOC."

"Roger that," said Rick.

* * *

The detectives returned to the EOC where Patty thanked all involved and provided a summary of occurrences at both houses. "We've got both of the local dealers, and busts at both houses resulted in no fatalities with only two injured. The injured were taken to Curry General before being booked. No law enforcement injured. This was a great success. My thanks to all of you and your agencies. Please enjoy coffee and the remaining pastries before leaving."

Patty and Rick remained for a while to visit with other members of the special task force.

Patty arrived first at the office and was hanging her jacket on the back of the chair when Rick walked in with a napkin over two pastries.

"Good meeting. Want one?" he asked.

Patty shook her head. "Thanks, but no. I enjoyed one this morning before we left, and it will be lunch time soon."

Rick chuckled. "You sound like a mother talking to her kids. Don't you ever get tired of being so practical?"

Patty looked at Rick unable to decide if he was teasing. "Why do you ask that?"

The words had come out of Rick's mouth before he could think about who he was talking with and what he'd said. "Uh, oh."

Patty continued to watch him. "Uh, oh, what? What do you mean?"

"I just meant that I should not have mentioned your practical nature. On second thought, it's a good nature. I mean, it's good to be practical. I understand your not wanting to spoil your lunch."

"No, you don't," said Patty. "You don't understand because you can eat whenever and whatever you want, and your system burns it. Every time I eat a pastry, I have to be willing to give up something else."

Rick lowered his hand holding the pastry he was about to bite into. "I didn't know that. And all these years I've been including something for you in my little white pastry bag. This means I've been the cause of your having to give up a lot!"

Patty sat quietly as Rick finished speaking. She waited for him to bite into his pastry and then continued the verbal exchange. "I've enjoyed the pastries you've brought in, and I've appreciated your thoughtfulness. It hasn't caused a problem for me."

Rick wiped the sugar off his mouth with a napkin. "Well, Patty, I'm relieved to hear that. It makes me feel much better. So that I can better understand your occasional dilemma, what would you have to give up if you ate this chocolate-covered old-fashioned doughnut I brought for you?"

Patty rolled her eyes. "Just forget it."

"No, Patty. I'm serious. We're partners and we should be aware of each other's sensitivities." Rick took another bite of his pastry and began speaking while chewing. "So, what would you have to give up?"

"I'd skip dessert after dinner or reduce my glass of wine to a half."

Rick nodded. "Well, now I understand why it's important for you to debate with yourself over whether to enjoy your favorite doughnut. I'd be more practical too if eating my pastry resulted in my giving up part of my dinner. I was concerned you were going to tell me that the reason you weren't enjoying your favorite doughnut was because you are concerned about your figure."

Rick and Patty's eyes locked. Rick smiled. "And I think there is absolutely nothing wrong with your figure. As a matter of fact, I rather like it."

A silence permeated the air throughout the office, broken only by the noises coming from the break room. Then Patty smiled. "I'll take that doughnut off your hands."

Twenty minutes later, Patty opened the Max Rainy file. "Is now a good time for us to discuss Rainy's interviews?"

Rick opened his file. "It is. Knowing what he did to Timothy might put a different spin on everything we've heard thus far. Like I mentioned yesterday, I've got a strong feeling we're missing something."

Patty nodded. "He told us nothing of any use the first time we interviewed him. And he was still denying knowing Jerry when we interviewed him the second time. Then he slipped up and said that he and Stuart weren't out that day. The words '*that day*' suggested he was speaking of a specific day. Of course, he later suggested it was just a slip of the tongue."

"We now know," said Rick, "that Max gave Jerry's knife and sheath to Peter Sham. And that everyone is afraid of Max, the one with the most fear being Peter. I figure his motive in giving Peter the knife was twofold. First, to scare him, knowing that Peter assumed Max probably killed Jerry. And secondly, to keep Peter quiet about Tim's beating."

Patty thumbed through several pages in her file. "Looking over these interviews, I don't read anything that's going to get us closer to the proof we need, or even clear circumstantial evidence."

Rick closed his file. "Max has a boat and he's a diver. That gives him the means and opportunity. But we are still left without a motive."

Patty wrote down a phone number from the file. "We've not been able to talk with Tim Rollins, but maybe we missed something with his parents. I'm going to set up an interview with them."

* * *

Mr. and Mrs. Rollins were agreeable to meeting with Patty and Rick that afternoon.

The detectives drove to Cave Junction. The Rollins' home was about a mile from the downtown area off Highway 199. The front gate was hanging off a hinge, and the lawn was overgrown. The house appeared as though no one cared.

Mrs. Rollins opened the door and invited the detectives in. She led them through the living room and into the small kitchen where Mr. Rollins sat at a table.

Patty looked around. There were dirty dishes in the sink, and the table was covered with crumbs. A cat slept on a towel in the corner. Mr. Rollins had a cane lying against his leg. In front of him was a coffee cup. Patty sat down next to him.

Rick sat across the table next to Mrs. Rollins. She didn't smile. Simply looked at Patty and asked, "What do you need from us?"

"We've learned what Max Rainy did to your son, and we are very sorry for the pain it's caused Timothy and both of you."

Mr. Rollins stared at his hands, folded on top of the table.

Mrs. Rollins nodded. "Thank you. Who told you?"

"We're not at liberty to tell you that, Mrs. Rollins. But we feel quite certain that the information we have is accurate. Max Rainy beat your son nearly to death. And Timothy didn't file a police report because he did not want his drug dealings made public. Is that about right?"

The couple looked at each other.

"That's right," she said. "And I suppose now that you know, you'll do nothing to bring Max Rainy to justice."

"On the contrary, Mrs. Rollins." Patty leaned forward. "Mrs. and Mr. Rollins, we are here because we believe that Max Rainy is a very bad man. We believe he needs to be taken off the street. Your son did not deserve what was done to him, and we're hoping we can stop Max before he does the same to someone else."

Tears formed in Mrs. Rollins' eyes, and one trickled down her cheek. "How can we help?"

Patty sat back in the chair. "We're having a difficult time coming up with a motive for Max to have killed Jerry Stengle. If we can convict Max on Jerry's murder and put him away for the next twenty or more years, we may be able to get someone to testify to Max's beating your son. The fear of retaliation from Max would be substantially reduced if we're successful. Do you understand?"

"Yes," she said. "I do. You want to know why Max might have killed Jerry."

"That's correct, Mrs. Rollins. Do you know of any reason from the time they were in school together for Max to hate Jerry?"

Mrs. Rollins nodded. "The accident."

Patty and Rick glanced at each other.

"What accident?" Patty asked.

Mr. Rollins looked up at his wife and nodded.

She continued. "It was when they were all in high school together. Max, Jerry, and our Timothy. Jerry got his driver's license. One evening he borrowed his dad's car. According to Timothy, Jerry picked him up and drove to Max's house. The three of them were going to the drive-in together. There were a lot of cars and a few trucks parked on the street. As Jerry drove past one of the trucks, Max's little sister ran out into the street, right in front of Jerry's car. He slammed on the brakes, but there was no way to avoid her. An ambulance was called, but she died on the way to the hospital. We learned later that the little girl was running across the street to play with a neighbor child."

Patty looked at Rick and he nodded slightly. She then returned her gaze to Mrs. Rollins.

"I'm sure that must have devastated Max's family."

Mrs. Rollins looked up. "And Jerry's. It made atheists out of some and alcoholics out of others. The sudden death of the girl forever altered the lives of everyone involved."

Patty glanced at Rick again and he leaned forward to ask a question.

"Mrs. Rollins, do you recall how the accident affected Max?"

"Well, our families have never been close, so I only know what Timothy told me. He said that Max became mean and angry. He missed a lot of school, and when he was there, he was belligerent toward the teachers and other students."

"Do you recall whether Timothy ever told you what, specifically, Max may have said to Jerry when he was acting out of anger?"

Mrs. Rollins stared at the top of the kitchen table. "Well, Tim said more than once that Max threatened Jerry. Max told Jerry that someday he'd pay for killing his sister."

Rick continued. "Was there a trial? Was Jerry punished?"

Mr. Rollins cleared his throat and looked up. "No. There was no need for a trial. It wasn't Jerry's fault. The girl ran into the street in front of him. There were witnesses, including our Tim. Max had no right to blame Jerry. Jerry already carried great sadness and guilt. It was just a horrible accident. But Max couldn't leave Jerry alone." Mr. Rollins looked into Rick's eyes. "Max needs to be locked up. He's not normal."

"Mr. Rollins," said Rick, "I heard that the reason Max attacked Timothy was due to Tim saying something about Max's sister. Do you know what it is Tim said?"

Mr. Rollins formed fists with both hands. "Yes, I do. Tim told Max that his sister's accident was her own fault."

Patty looked at Rick and then back to the broken couple. "What you've told us today will help in our effort to find Jerry's killer and hold Max Rainy responsible for his attack on Tim."

Mr. Rollins glanced at his wife and then at Patty. "Do you have any absolute proof that Max killed Jerry?"

"We can't talk about an ongoing investigation, Mr. Rollins."

Mr. Rollins balled his fists up again. "I'll take that as a no. I have another question. You've spoken with everyone who might know whether Max killed Jerry. Have any of those people agreed to talk about the murder?"

"I'm sorry, Mr. Rollins. I can't answer that."

Mr. Rollins got up slowly and walked out of the room.

Patty put her business card on the table. "Thank you, Mrs. Rollins. Call me if you think of anything else that might be helpful. We can see ourselves out."

Patty and Rick left Cave Junction for Brookings.

Rick hit the steering wheel with the palm of his hand. "That's our missing piece of the puzzle. Jerry's responsibility for the accident gives Max motive. And you know, we should have figured this out sooner. Randy Stengle mentioned something about a serious accident when we first interviewed him. He mentioned it as one of the reasons why Max became so messed up in high school. We should have asked him more about the accident."

"It does give him motive," said Patty, "but we still can't link him to the murder. We've got to find evidence of peanut oil and or succinylcholine. Let's find out where he keeps his boat. I'll get a search warrant. The judge may give me one telephonically based upon this new information."

At the office, Patty put in a call to the courthouse and scheduled a time for her telephonic search warrant request. The conference call included the judge, Patty, Rick, and the court stenographer. For the accuracy of the written transcript, each stated their name prior to every statement they made. Patty shared the information she and Rick had learned from Mr. and Mrs. Rollins.

The judge listened, then asked, "How certain are you that you'll find the evidence you need on the boat?"

"I'm not certain at all, Your Honor. But Rick and I are convinced Max murdered Jerry Stengle. And he had to have stored the peanut oil and the drug somewhere. We have no leads, and therefore we're going through a process of elimination."

The judge then provided his final statement. "In consideration of all of the information provided, I order Detectives Patty O'Toole and Rick Starker to search the boat belonging to Max Rainy."

"Thank you, Your Honor. This is very much appreciated."

"You're welcome, Detective O'Toole." The judge paused. "Before you go, Detective."

"Yes, Your Honor?"

"This will be the last search warrant associated with Rainy without some additional evidence."

"I understand, Your Honor."

Patty ended the call. "I'll call the Sheriff and let him know what we've got. Then we should leave."

Rick nodded. Patty made the call, and the detectives left for the port. "I've got a question about another subject."

Patty leaned back in her chair. "Yes?"

"Have you heard of gorse?"

"Of course. There's quite a bit of it in our part of the state. Why do you ask?"

"I read in the paper that the City of Brookings is asking homeowners to destroy any of it they find on their property. So I googled it and discovered just how dangerous it is. Gorse was the cause of a major fire that consumed Bandon in 1936. The town's founder planted it all around his newly-established coastal community, not knowing that the oily plant loves fire."

"I know of that fire," said Patty. "It had to have been horrible. Some residents reported that when the fire hit the gorse, flames shot up in the air as though gasoline had been poured on the bush. They discovered that water wouldn't put out the fire."

"Well," said Rick, "that fire consumed Bandon, and it's estimated that ten people were killed. The article I read reported that people are attempting all the time to eliminate gorse here on the coast, but such efforts have not been completely successful."

Brad walked into the office. "Do you two want help?"

"No, thanks, Brad. I let the Sheriff know what we plan to do, and he's going to loan us a deputy since his substation is at the port."

Rick stood up and touched his gun with his elbow. Patty put her jacket on.

"I'll drive," said Rick.

Patty smiled. "I know. I'll let Deputy Snowden know that we're on our way. Let's hope we'll find that Max is hiding something on his fishing vessel."

Patty and Rick arrived at the port and walked over to the Sheriff's substation. The volunteer at the front desk welcomed them.

"May I help you?"

"No, thank you. We're here to see Deputy Snowden."

Before the volunteer could say any more, the deputy walked out of the patrol office and joined the detectives.

"I know the boat," he said.

The three of them walked down the ramp to the dock and saw Max on the boat.

Max looked up. "Oh, no. What, now?"

"Good afternoon, Max," greeted Patty. "We're here to search your boat. Is there anyone else on board?"

Max's eyes grew large as he hollered at the detectives. "Search my boat? You people don't give up, do you? This is harassment, and I'm going to sue!"

Patty quietly asked again. "Is there anyone else on the boat, Max?"

"No. It's just me."

Rick stepped down onto the boat while addressing Max. "Wait on the dock until we're done."

Max stepped onto the dock, and Patty gave him a copy of the warrant. The deputy remained on the dock while Rick and Patty searched the small boat.

Patty opened a partially-hidden storage compartment. "Rick? There's a greasy spot in here, as though something was spilled. What does it smell like to you?"

Rick put his nose close to the compartment opening. "Peanuts. That smells like peanut oil."

"I agree," said Patty. "I want to get forensics in here to take a sample and photos. I also want them to check for Jerry's fingerprints." She turned to Max.

"We're going to take custody of your boat, Max, which means you can't return to it until we're done."

Max turned beet-red and began to pace back and forth. "Your warrant doesn't give you the right to do that."

"Yes, it does," said Patty, "and finding peanut oil on your boat adds to it."

Max threw his arms in the air. "Peanut oil? That's from the jar of peanut butter I took out with me last week. It must have fallen over."

"We'll have someone down here tomorrow to dust your boat for prints and take a sample of that oil. Are we going to find Jerry's prints, Max?"

"You're not going to find anything more than you did at my house. And that was nothing. I can't believe you won't let me back on my boat! Why don't you spend your time looking for the real killer?" He began walking off.

Rick called out, "Don't leave town, Max."

Max threw his head back. "I can't. You have my boat."

Patty asked Deputy Snowden if he could bring a couple of the Sheriff's "No Trespassing" signs down to the boat. She also asked if it might be possible for a couple of the reserve deputies to keep an eye on the boat until a forensic tech could arrive the following morning. The deputy said he'd take care of it. Patty thanked him, and the detectives started back to their office.

Patty's cell phone rang. She saw it was her mother. "Detective O'Toole."

"Hello, Detective O'Toole. This is your mother."

Patty smiled. "How's your day going, Mom?"

"It's going fine. I spent time with Grace this morning. We walked on the beach and enjoyed a cup of coffee together."

"That's great, Mom. How is Grace doing?"

"She's okay. There's a heaviness about her that I can't quite put my finger on. Like a deep sadness. I think she works hard to compensate for it with humor. It's admirable."

"Well, Mom, I'm glad she has you for a friend. I'm sure she appreciates having someone she can trust to talk with."

"You know, dear, I think you're right. Each time we talk she shares a little bit more. I enjoy her company too. She's interesting. She worked in the banking industry for many years managing and selling property referred to as REOs. That stands for 'real estate owned.' I'll share one of her stories with you the next time we're together.

"Now, enough about me. Tell me about you and Rick. Do you know how the diver died? Are you looking for a murderer? Is it someone local?"

"I can't talk about it now, Mom, but I'll let you know when I can. Say hello to Bill for me."

"Okay, dear. You tell Rick 'hi' for me."

"Will do, Mom."

"Oh, Patty. I almost forgot the reason I called. Our HOA is holding a garage sale in a couple of weeks. Bill helped me to get four big boxes of stuff out of the garage. Can you come over and help me go through them and find items that I can donate to our association's auction?"

"Sure, Mom. I'll let you know tomorrow morning when I can drop by."

"That will be great, Patty. Bye for now. Love you."

"Love you too, Mom."

Rick was answering voicemail messages when Patty finished her call. He finished up and saw that Patty was free. "Your mom okay?"

"She is. I know it helps her to talk with me every day or so. She hasn't always had such a need. I think it has to do with her age."

Rick nodded. "That's understandable." He put the file he'd been working on away in his desk. "I'm calling it a day. See you tomorrow."

"Yeah. I've got a few emails to answer, then I'll be on my way too."

Rick walked out to the unmarked car, got in, and sat down. He scrolled down his contact list and stopped at Stella's name. Then he put the phone in his pocket and drove to the evening AA meeting.

CHAPTER NINETEEN

Oscar barked when Patty rang the doorbell. Bill greeted his stepdaughter and invited her in. "Good morning. Glad you could make it over to help your mom. She's been going through a few boxes and is already having a difficult time deciding what to give up."

Patty smiled. "I thought that might be the case. How are you?"

"Enjoying my enhanced world of sound. These hearing aids have given me a whole new appreciation for life around me. I wish I'd purchased them several years ago. Would have saved Maggie and me a number of frustrating moments."

Patty lightly put her hand on Bill's arm. "And a few humorous ones too, from what Mom has told me."

Bill laughed. "That too."

Oscar barked again, and Patty reached down to pet him. Oscar turned over on his back so that Patty could rub his tummy.

"You do know, Patty, that doing that makes you Oscar's best bud."

Patty laughed. "I can see that."

Maggie walked into the room and gave her daughter a hug. "Hello, dear."

"Hi, Mom. Bill tells me you're already going through boxes."

"I am, and I'm glad you're here to help. Bill helped me bring them in from the garage, and we set them in the spare room. Come look."

Patty followed her mother down the hall. "You've got quite a bit of stuff stacked up on the bed, Mom. Do you want me to help you price it?"

"Oh, no, dear. That's the stuff from the first two boxes I opened. I held each item and remembered where it came from, and I can't part with any of it."

Patty picked up a knitted baby sweater and cap.

Maggie nodded toward the knitted pieces. "Those were yours," she said. "Your Grandmother Lee made them for you. They bring precious memories to me."

Patty set down the baby clothes. "I understand, Mom. But what about this tablecloth?"

Maggie took the cloth from her daughter's hands. "That was the first table-cloth your dad and I bought after we were married. It covered a small table in the apartment we rented. The candle holders you see were also some of the first things we purchased for our home. They bring me wonderful memories."

Patty picked up the candle holders. "These are beautiful, Mom. It's a shame to keep them boxed up."

"I know, dear, but Bill and I don't have room for a lot of extra things. Would you want them?"

"I'd love to have them, Mom. They'll have special meaning to me, knowing that they were used by you and Dad."

"That makes me very happy, Patty. You take whatever you'd like from these things. I'll pack the rest of it again and ask Bill to return the boxes to the garage. We'll just make a cash donation to the cause."

"Sounds like a great idea, Mom. I have a little time. Would you like for me to help you pack these items back into their boxes? I'd like to hear more stories about where these treasures came from."

Maggie's eyes teared up. "I would like that, dear."

CHAPTER TWENTY

Patty's cell phone rang. She looked at caller ID and got Rick's attention. "It's the lab. I'll put it on speaker. This is Detective O'Toole."

"Good morning, Detective. This is Hal Quincy. I'm a forensic tech with the lab. I've got the results of our boat search."

"We've been looking forward to hearing from you, Mr. Quincy. I'm here with Detective Starker, and I have you on speaker phone. What can you tell us?"

"We found two prints on the boat that match those of the deceased diver, Jerry Stengle."

Patty looked at Rick, lifted her right arm, bent it at the elbow, pulled it straight down, and whispered, "Yes."

Rick smiled. "That's great. And the oil?"

"I can tell you that the substance we collected is definitely peanut oil. We cannot confirm whether it came from the same container as the oil on the deceased's mouthpiece."

Patty responded, "That's great news, Mr. Quincy. The fingerprints give us what we need to arrest the responsible. The peanut oil will help with our circumstantial evidence."

"Glad I could be of some help," said Quincy.

"You've been a great help. Thank you."

Patty ended the call. "I've got to let the LT know. Will you ask Brad to bring Rainy in? We can talk to him here before he's taken up north."

Rick phoned Brad.

Patty walked down the hall. As always, the lieutenant greeted her as she walked through his office door.

"Hello, O'Toole. Judging from the smile on your face, I'd say you have good news."

"I do, LT. We can arrest Max Rainy. Jerry's fingerprints are on the boat, and the lab confirmed the substance we found is peanut oil."

"In addition to the lab results, we've discovered a motive for Max to have murdered Jerry. While in high school, Max's younger sister was killed in an automobile accident. Jerry was driving the car. The accident was deemed to be the child's fault, but Max was overheard saying that he would kill Jerry."

The lieutenant nodded. "Good work, O'Toole. Maybe you can get him to confess if he sees his alibi falling apart. There are still loose ends, though, and until you can find evidence of the succinylcholine, you've got a missing piece to the puzzle. Find that piece and there will be no chance of Max Rainy going free."

Patty's smile faded. "Rick and I will find it, LT. We're close. We both feel it. But we can now lock Max up while we continue to investigate."

"Yes, and that's good, O'Toole."

Patty walked back down the hall. She let Rick know the lieutenant agreed with their plan to arrest Max while continuing to investigate.

A few minutes had passed when Patty's cell phone rang. "Hey, Brad. Did you find Rainy at this home?"

"We did, Patty. You and Rick need to get over here."

"Why? Is he putting up a fight?"

"He's not doing anything, Patty. Max Rainy is dead."

Patty paused as she stared at Rick, then continued to talk to Brad. "We're on our way. Keep everyone out."

Rick was already on his feet and ready to go when Patty ended the call with Brad. "The look on your face tells me this isn't good news."

"He's dead."

Rick gave Patty a puzzled look. "Who?"

"Rainy. He's dead. Let's go."

Brad met the detectives at the front door and pointed toward the kitchen. "He's in there."

Patty and Rick slipped on their cloth booties and nitrile gloves, and walked into the kitchen. Lying on the floor was their prime suspect for the murder of Jerry Stengle. Max Rainy lay on his back with a dive spear through his chest.

Patty loudly exhaled. "How many people do you think wanted Max Rainy dead?"

Rick stared at the body. "I can think of at least a half-dozen."

"At least," said Patty. "I'll call Doc Miller and let the LT know. You want to direct Brad on securing the premises?" Rick nodded.

Patty called the medical examiner.

"Greetings, Detective O'Toole. Is this a business call or are you checking up on me?"

"The former, Doc. Our prime suspect for the succinylcholine murder is lying on his kitchen floor with a dive spear through his chest."

"A dive spear. How interesting. But not unique. Takes me back a few years when I examined another such death. A couple of divers separated and lost track of one another. One saw a fish he wanted. His spear went through the fish and into his dive partner who had been hidden by seaweed. A tragic accident. I'm guessing you think this was no accident."

"You guess right, Doc."

"Okay, have him moved to the funeral home, and I'll be out later today."

"Let us know when you have an ETA, Doc, and we'll have someone pick you up at the airport."

"Will do, Detective."

Patty called the lieutenant and informed him of Rainy's death.

The lieutenant listened and paused before responding. "You and Rick can handle this, O'Toole. In addition to your continued search for the drug used to kill your diver. The murder of Rainy has now become your priority. Have you considered where you'll start?"

"I have, LT. We'll interview Peter Sham and go from there with the same persons of interest we interviewed for the death of Stengle."

"That's a good plan. One of those men could be Rainy's killer. Be careful, O'Toole."

"We will, LT."

Patty checked with Rick that he and Brad had communicated on securing the premises and starting a log. She called the jail and set up an interview with Peter Sham, and asked one of the patrol deputies to bring Stuart in for questioning. Neither Peter nor Stuart were to be told of Rainy's death.

Rick walked into the office with coffee and set a mug down on Patty's desk. "I'm going back for cake. Want some?"

"I would, thanks. We've got a long day ahead of us, and I think I'm going to need the sugar."

Rick returned with a plate in each hand and handed Patty her cake. "Well, this changes plan A. Want to talk about B?"

Patty set the cake down and picked up her fork. "I do. We know Sham couldn't have done it, but he might loosen up now that Max is dead. I saw Brad in the hall. He said Stuart's been spotted. We also need to talk with Randy Stengle. What are your thoughts on Connor and Trevor?"

"They are certainly persons of interest."

"Got a best guess on who speared Rainy?"

Rick set down his fork. "I've been thinking about that. It has to be someone with knowledge about operating the diving apparatus. And someone who knows where Max lives."

Patty swallowed. "I agree. Doc Miller will be able to tell us whether there are any defensive wounds. I find it hard to believe that the killer could have loaded the gun without Rainy becoming suspicious. Therefore, Rainy knew his assailant, or the killer caught Rainy by surprise."

"What if the killer was in the house when Rainy arrived home?" asked Rick. "The gun could have been loaded, providing no opportunity for Rainy to escape his assailant."

"That's the most logical scenario," said Patty. "Max would have had no time to react. That also suggests that the killer had a key to Rainy's home."

"So, to answer your question," said Rick, "I'm guessing it was Stuart."

Patty sliced her fork into another piece of cake. "Why Stuart?"

"Because. Stuart fears Max and knows that Max killed Jerry and attacked Timothy. He's scared, but, unlike Peter, I think that Stuart would have the courage to face Max as long as he didn't have to worry about being attacked himself."

Brad called Patty. "Stuart was picked up at Macklyn Cove. He's in the interview room."

"Thanks, Brad. We'll be there in a minute." She looked at Rick.

"I agree with you about Stuart. Let's find out whether we still feel this way after his reaction to our news."

Rick stood up. "How do you want to do this?"

"I'll lead. If needed, you come in as bad cop."

As the detectives entered the room, Stuart sat nervously on the opposite side of the table. He was rubbing his knees with his hands again, as though attempting to wipe off the sweat.

"Why am I here?"

Patty ignored the question. "Where have you been today, Stuart?"

"Why are you asking me that? Your officers picked me up at Macklyn Cove. They know where I've been, and I'm sure they told you."

"What time did you get to the cove?"

"I don't remember exactly. Sometime before noon."

"Be more exact."

"I got up about ten and drove over to the cove to fish."

"Was Max up when you left?"

"I don't know. We don't check with each other before leaving the house."

"Did you eat breakfast before leaving the house?"

Stuart looked at Patty and then to Rick. "What is this about? Why are you asking if I ate breakfast? Why did you bring me in here?"

"Do you know whether Max spent the night at home?"

"I don't know where he slept. He could have been home or at his mother's since he sees her every day. Now I want to leave. If you want to know more about Max, you'll have to ask him."

Patty leaned forward. "We can't do that, Stuart."

Stuart nodded. "I know, because he's tired of your questions too."

Patty continued. "We can't ask Max questions, Stuart, because Max Rainy is dead."

Stuart's jaw dropped, and he leaned back in his chair. "What? You're lying. Trying to make me talk."

"No, Stuart. We're not lying. Max was found dead in his kitchen this morning."

Stuart sat upright again and shook his head from side to side. "How?"

"He was shot with a speargun. His own speargun."

Stuart's eyes opened wide as he processed the information. "How? I mean, who? Do you know who killed him?"

"Not yet," said Patty. "Who do you know has a key to Max's house?"

"Other than me? Probably three or four people who rented his spare room before me."

"Do you know anyone who might have wanted Max Rainy dead?"

Stuart laughed. "You're kidding, right? Lots of people hated Max, with good reason. He wasn't a friendly guy."

"Then why did you hang out with him?"

Stuart shrugged. "He had a boat and a room to rent. And once he had you in his debt, you didn't tell Max no."

Patty glanced at Rick and leaned back in her chair.

Rick leaned forward. "Who are the others who rented from Max?" Rick wrote down the names as Stuart recalled them. "Peter, Tim, and Connor. Maybe Trevor, I don't know for sure."

Patty spoke up. "Timothy? Why would Tim have rented a room from Max?"

"Tim got a job on one of the fishing boats and rented from Max to avoid the commute. It was only for a couple of weeks because he and Max got into it about something. Anyway, Tim moved out and in with his parents in Cave Junction."

Rick looked into Stuart's eyes. "Do you spearfish?"

"Yes."

"Does it take special skill to know how to load and shoot it?"

"Well, I don't know that it takes a special skill, but you do need to be careful."

"Is there any reason we shouldn't arrest you for Max's death?"

"Yeah. I didn't do it. I have no interest in spending my life behind bars. I can't say I'm sorry he's dead, though."

"We're getting closer to learning who killed Jerry, Stuart, and we believe you know that it was Max. He's dead now and can't do anything to you. It will help your case if you come clean and talk to us."

Stuart smiled slightly. "I don't know who killed Jerry. If Max did it, you can't prove I was anywhere near him when it happened."

"What about the abalone?"

Stuart turned red. "What abalone?"

"The abalone we found in the freezer you and Max share. Jerry's brother told us that Max invited Jerry to go abalone-diving. You were with them, Stuart. Did you take care of the abalone while Max killed Jerry?"

Stuart paused before answering. "I don't fish for abalone because it's illegal, and I didn't have anything to do with Jerry's murder. I'm done talking."

Patty and Rick stood up and started for the door. Patty stopped and turned around to speak again with Stuart. "You'll be charged and convicted with being an accessory to murder. You'll spend years in prison. Admitting your involvement now may shave a few years off your sentence. Max is dead, so there's no chance of retaliation from him if you tell us what happened. Think about it, Stuart. Talking to us is your only chance."

Brad walked Stuart back to the reception room.

After returning to the office, Rick leaned back in his chair and stared out the window. Patty looked at him and asked, "Thinking about Stuart's responses?"

"No. But I am thinking about the case."

Patty waited for Rick to continue. "Something you want to talk about with me?"

Rick turned and looked at Patty. "Have you noticed how often we've heard that Max visits his mother?"

Patty nodded. "I have. She's evidently housebound, and Max had to deliver medication to her."

Rick was silent as he continued to stare at Patty. Then she broke the silence. "Shoot. We need to check out the mother."

Patty got an address off the internet for a Rosemary Rainy. She and Rick drove across town.

The address was for a small park model in a residential area off the high-way. The park was nicely landscaped and well-maintained except for Mrs. Rainy's home. The yard hadn't been tended for some time, and the screen door had a tear in it. The detectives walked up to the front door.

Rick knocked on the door. He and Patty waited, and Rick knocked again. They walked to the back where the yard was similarly unkept and tried the door. After walking completely around the outside of the house, they were greeted by a middle-aged man. He held a leash in his hand. At the other end was a small white dog. He smiled at the detectives. "May I be of help?"

"Thank you," said Patty. "I'm Detective O'Toole and this is Detective Starker. Are you a neighbor?"

The man pointed down the street. "Yes. I live in the yellow house there. My name is David Gray."

"Hello, Mr. Gray. We're looking for Rosemary Rainy. She doesn't seem to be home now or can't come to the door. Do you know how we might reach her?"

The man shook his head. "Not unless you're psychic."

"Oh, has she moved?"

The man looked up at the house. "No, she hasn't moved. Rosemary died."

Patty glanced at Rick and returned her attention to the neighbor. "Do you know when she died?"

The man brought his hand up and rubbed his chin. "Well, it must be about three years ago now."

Rick took notes while Patty continued. "Has this place sat vacant since her death?"

The little dog yelped. "Not exactly," said the man as he lifted the dog into his arms. "I mean, to my knowledge it hasn't sold. But a young guy goes in and out almost daily."

Rick looked up from his notepad. "Do you know this young guy's name and relation to Mrs. Rainy?"

The man petted his dog. "I spoke with him a few months after Rosemary died. He said he was her son. He always picks up mail, stays for a couple of hours, and leaves."

Rick asked again. "He give you his name?"

The man put the little dog back down on its feet. "You know, he did when I first met him. I don't recall now what it was. It was short. Maybe, Rex or Mick."

"What about Max?"

The man smiled. "Yes, that was it. He said his name was Max Rainy."

"Thank you," said Patty. The neighbor began to walk away when Patty called to him again. "You wouldn't happen to know how Rosemary Rainy died?"

The man turned and looked at Patty. "All I heard was that she drowned. It was odd."

"Why's that?" asked Patty.

"Because she drowned in her own bathtub. Rosemary golfed four times a week and was quite active with our senior center. Why would a perfectly healthy woman drown in her bathtub?"

Patty let the question go. "Thank you, Mr. Gray."

CHAPTER TWENTY-ONE

Patty and Rick returned to their office. Patty leaned over and pulled a form from a file in her drawer. "I'll complete the affidavit for a search warrant. Will you ask Brad to confirm Rosemary Rainy's death? Once confirmed, we need to get into her house."

Rick nodded and picked up his phone. "Seems Jerry Stengle may not have been Max's first victim. I wonder how many more are out there?"

Patty cringed. "That's a frightening thought." Patty's cell phone buzzed and caller ID showed it was Doc Miller calling. "Hello, Doc."

"Hi, Detective O'Toole. You sound a bit out of breath."

"That's because I am. We've got a lot going on."

"Well, I don't want to slow down the law. Your victim, Max Rainy, has no defensive wounds and nothing under his fingernails that might suggest he put up any kind of a struggle."

"That's what we expected, Doc. Thanks for the confirmation."

"You getting close to cracking the case?"

"That depends upon which case you're asking about, Doc. Investigating the death of Jerry Stengle has taken several unexpected turns. We're closing in on the Stengle death. But Rainy's murderer is still an unknown, and we've just learned that his mother died three years ago under what Rick and I consider to be suspicious circumstances. Mrs. Rainy, a highly active woman, drowned in her bathtub."

The doc laughed quietly. "It's good to know that you and Rick are the investigating detectives on these cases. Makes me feel that the world is a little bit safer. You and Rick take care."

"Thanks, Doc, for the vote of confidence and the good wishes. You take care too."

Rick was waiting to learn what the doc has reported and looked up when he heard Patty end the call. She put her phone down. "As we expected. No defensive wounds or signs of a struggle. Did you talk with Brad?"

"Yeah. He should have an answer for us any minute now."

"I need to get this affidavit to the judge. Hopefully, he can see me today." Patty called the court clerk. "This is Detective O'Toole and I have a search warrant affidavit. I'd like to see the judge as soon as possible." She explained the reason for her urgency.

"Hold on, Detective."

Patty waited for several minutes before the clerk came back on the line.

"Bring your affidavit in, Detective. If you can get here within the next thirty minutes, the judge can see you. If not, I'll need to schedule you for tomorrow morning."

"I'll be there within the next thirty minutes," said Patty. She quickly grabbed her purse and let Rick know her thoughts. "I believe the judge will give us the warrant after hearing how close we are."

Patty walked into the courthouse with five minutes to spare in the time-frame she'd promised and was directed into the judge's chambers. Her communication with the judge included information about the deaths of Max Rainy and his mother. Patty related how Max had consistently told his friends that he went to his mother's home to deliver much-needed medicine to her.

The judge asked a few questions and signed the requested warrant.

"Thank you, Your Honor."

"You're welcome, Detective. This is good work on the part of you and Detective Starker. I hope you find what you need."

Before leaving the courthouse, Patty called Rick to let him know she had the warrant. "Will you call a locksmith and ask him to meet us there in forty minutes? I'll let the jail know that we won't interview Peter Sham until tomorrow."

"I'll do that. Brad got back to me on Rosemary Rainy. I'm looking at a copy of the death certificate. I've done a bit of research, and since her property went through probate, I can tell you that she left her house to Max."

"That's not a surprise," said Patty. "And it wouldn't be a surprise to learn that he's been living off the equity. Our call's going to drop soon, so let's continue our discussion at the office."

Patty walked into the office to find Rick sipping on a cup of coffee. She laid her things on her desk and sat down. "You know, Rick, I was thinking on the drive down here about the past murder cases we've worked on together and solved. I figure we've dealt with some of the worst of mankind. And Max Rainy's part of the same lot."

Rick nodded and stood up. "I agree. And just thinking about those past cases makes me hungry." He walked out of the office and returned a couple of minutes later with several cookies. "Chocolate chip. You want a few?"

"I'll take one."

Rick picked up one of the cookies and put it on Patty's desk. "Only one?"

Patty smiled. "First cake and now cookies. I'll need another bike ride soon to burn this off."

"How about a hike this time?" asked Rick. "I'll plan it, and I'll bring a picnic lunch."

Patty put the cookie down. "You're going to prepare a picnic lunch?"

Rick drank some coffee and put his mug down. "I didn't say I'd prepare it. I said that I'd bring it. I know of a couple places in town that make great deli sandwiches."

"That sounds delicious. When do you want to do this?"

The detectives locked eyes, and Rick responded. "As soon as we wrap up Jerry Stengle's murder or a couple weeks from now, whichever is sooner."

Patty swallowed. "I'll look forward to it." She took another bite of her cookie. "We need to get on with our search. Something tells me we're going to find the succinylcholine."

CHAPTER TWENTY-TWO

The detectives drove to the house where the locksmith was waiting. As is required, Rick knocked loudly on the front door. "Police. We have a search warrant. Open the door." He then directed the locksmith to open the door. Patty and Rick walked in to find the place somewhat tidy except for the kitchen. The sink was full of unwashed dishes.

"Where do you want to start?" asked Rick.

"If he had the drug, he'd probably have kept it in the garage. We can go from there."

The garage was attached to the house and was entered through a door off the living room. When the detectives walked in, they found an older model Ford Escort. Pieces of diving equipment lay on a small workbench attached to the back wall. Shelves lined one side of the room. Several cardboard boxes were stored on them.

Patty walked over to the workbench, which was cluttered with objects. She scanned what was there, moving her gaze from left to right. Pliers, hammer, flashlight, and a file. "Rick?"

Rick was moving boxes on one of the shelves. "Yeah?"

"You need to take a look at this."

Rick walked over to the workbench.

Patty pointed to a partially-full jar of peanut butter. There was still a layer of peanut oil visible. Next to the jar lay a small brush that appeared to be covered with an oily substance. The detectives' eyes continued to scan across the bench and stopped. A large glass jar held several syringes, two of which were full of liquid.

"This could be it, Rick. This could be what we've been looking for."

Rick took several photos of the workbench and the items sitting on top. "I'll go to the car and get evidence bags and a box."

"While you do that, I'll take a look inside." Patty walked through the kitchen and down the hall to one of two bedrooms. The bed was unmade. Men's clothes were strewn about on the floor. The closet door was open. Patty could see that whoever used the room had little use for hangers. Scanning over to the bedside table she saw a dive knife and mask, and across the room she spotted a computer on a corner desk.

Rick walked up to the doorway. "I've got photos. The peanut butter jar and syringes are secured in the car."

"We'll need another box, Rick. Judging from the clothes and dive items, I'm guessing this was Max's room. Which means this was his computer."

Rick nodded. "I'll get another evidence box from the car, but let's finish searching the house first. I may need to bring in more than one box."

Patty followed Rick out. "I'll look at the second bedroom and bath. You can take the kitchen."

The second bedroom was clearly decorated for a feminine taste. The bed was covered with a floral chenille bedspread. Lace curtains framed a large picture window. A photo of a woman standing next to a young girl sat on the bedside table next to a small lamp.

Patty checked the closet and walked down the hall to the bathroom. She opened the medicine cabinet. Her gaze immediately went to the bottom shelf, where a used syringe lay. She left it alone and joined Rick in the kitchen.

"I've got a syringe in the bathroom medicine cabinet."

"A syringe?" asked Rick. "That's a surprise, given Max was so careful about covering up Jerry's death. Why wouldn't he get rid of the syringe if he used it to kill his mother?"

"That's a good question. His mother's bedroom looks untouched since her death. Maybe keeping the syringe was a reminder to Max of the reason he killed her if, in fact, he did. Their relationship could not have been what we consider to be normal, considering that he didn't clean the room after she'd passed. Your question is one for a forensic psychologist. We'll need photos before we bag the syringe. You find anything in here?"

"Not what we're looking for, but Max was using this freezer as the over-flow for his abalone. No sign of peanut butter, drugs, or drug paraphernalia. What about the second bedroom?"

"The second bedroom had to have been hers, based upon the décor. There is a photo on her bedstand, and it's a picture of a woman and a young girl. I expect it is of Mrs. Rainy and the daughter she lost. No photo of Max. That kind of tells a story."

"You know," said Rick, "I'm wondering why the syringe wasn't found when Mrs. Rainy died."

"I wondered the same thing when I saw it. But then, if Mrs. Rainy's death was assumed accidental, there would have been no search for a murder weapon."

"That makes sense," said Rick. "I'll go to the car and get a box for the computer and a container for the syringe. Finding it may result in the exhumation of Mrs. Rainy's body. An accidental drowning would not have gone to Doc Miller."

"No," said Patty. "And if she were seen by a deputy medical examiner, the DME would have been there solely for the purpose of confirming death. A small hole between her fingers would not have been noticed."

Rick tilted his head. "And far less chance of being noticed if Max waited a few days before calling in the death."

"Well, let's get back to the office so that we can have the evidence sent off to the lab. We can take the computer and attempt to get into it at the station. If that doesn't work, we'll send it to the state lab for their IT department."

Rick smiled at Patty. "We hit the jackpot here."

She returned the smile. "I think so too, Rick. I think we've got what we need to solve Jerry's murder. However, we've also discovered one, possibly two additional murders. Our investigation needs to turn to who killed Max Rainy, and then we need to learn whether Rosemary Rainy was a victim of her son."

* * *

Rick took care of sending evidence to the lab while Patty dusted the computer for prints and opened it to determine if there was a password.

"No password required, Rick. I'm going to type in 'succinylcholine' in the search bar." Thirty seconds later, she summoned Rick. "You've got to see this."

Rick looked up from his desk. "Was Max researching the drug?"

"He was doing a lot more than research. There's an invoice for succinylcholine."

Rick stood up. "An invoice? Let me see. My research suggested there was no way for an individual to purchase the drug in the U.S."

"Yeah, but he didn't purchase it in the U.S."

Rick looked at the computer. "Mexico! Mr. Rainy was far more savvy about illegal drug purchasing than I gave him credit for."

Patty looked up at Rick. "So our instincts were right all along. It was Max who killed Jerry. This invoice and a positive ID on the substance we're submitting to the lab should be all we need."

Rick walked over to the window. "It may be all we need for Stuart to talk too."

"How about we talk to Peter first, Rick? Give him a chance to reduce his sentence. I'm guessing this will be a turning point in his life."

"Okay with me. But I wouldn't think too highly of Peter Sham. He has a low opinion of himself which, in part, is how he found himself in the company of Max Rainy. That doesn't portend well for a clean lifestyle."

"I know what you're saying, but I'd like for Peter to have a second chance if he remains a model prisoner. I'll call the jail and set up our interview."

Rick's cell phone vibrated. He walked over to his desk, picked up the phone, and looked at caller ID. He answered while walking back over to the window. "Detective Starker."

"Hi, Rick. It's Stella. Is this a good time to talk?"

Rick turned and saw that Patty was still on the phone with the jail. "Sure."

"Well, I've been doing a lot of thinking since living with my sister and her kids. And I'm missing you. I'm thinking about moving back to Brookings."

Stella stopped talking, and Rick listened to the silence before responding. "It's only been a few weeks since you moved, Stella. That's hardly enough time for you to know what you want."

"I guess what I'm saying, Rick, is that I don't need more time. I want to be with you. I'd like for us to get to know each other better. How does that sound to you? Do you want to be with me?"

Rick looked over at Patty again. "I'm sorry, Stella, but it wouldn't be a good idea for us to get together. I've had time to think too since you left, and my life is taking a turn that I'm feeling pretty good about."

"Oh. So you're already dating someone else. That was fast. Or were you seeing her when you told me you wanted to date me?"

"I genuinely meant everything I said to you, Stella, but my dating circumstances have changed, and I like where I'm at right now. I wish the best for you and hope that you find what you're looking for."

"Okay, Rick. Well, give me a call if you change your mind. I could be out there in two days."

"Take care, Stella."

Rick ended the call and looked up to find Patty watching him. She smiled slightly before commenting on her call.

"We can see Peter Sham this afternoon. Want to get some lunch and then head up to Gold Beach?"

"I'm starving."

CHAPTER TWENTY-THREE

Peter Sham sat at the table with his handcuffs secured to an iron ring. Patty and Rick sat across from him with their backs to the one-way window.

Patty took the lead. "Hi, Peter."

Peter looked tired and had dark circles under his eyes. He also appeared to have lost weight. He spoke quietly. "Hi."

Patty set a can of Coke on the table. "It's yours if you want it."

Peter shook his head. "No, thanks."

Patty left the can. "How are you doing in here, Peter?"

Peter looked at Patty and then at Rick. "Okay."

"You don't look okay. You look tired and like you've lost weight. Did you see the doctor about that cut over your eyebrow?"

Peter tipped his head down. "What do you want?"

"We've come with news that we believe will be good news for you, Peter."

Peter did not respond.

"We've come to tell you that Max Rainy is dead."

Several seconds went by without any response from Peter. He then slowly raised his head. "How?"

"Someone shot him with a speargun. Max's speargun. A couple of our officers found him on the kitchen floor."

Peter slowly nodded his head as though processing what he'd just been told.

"Do you know what this means, Peter?"

Patty waited and continued when there was no response. "It means you can tell us about Max killing Jerry. It means you can tell us what you know and most probably reduce your sentence. You would like to reduce your sentence, wouldn't you, Peter?"

Peter continued to sit quietly, his gaze wavering between the top of the table and Patty.

"He can't hurt you now, Peter. When you get out of here, you can start over again and stay on the right side of the law. You can get a job and take care of yourself without Max looking over your shoulder."

The young man's silence continued. Rick motioned to Patty that he had something to say.

"Look, Peter, Detective O'Toole seems to think there's something good in you. I'm not so sure. But she thinks that, if given the chance, you'll give up the drugs and start living a clean life. Detective O'Toole wants to talk to the DA about shaving off some of your sentence in exchange for your telling us what happened to Jerry Stengle. She also requires that you promise to remain clean and get a job once you're out. Like I said, you're still a question mark for me."

The detectives waited for Peter's response, but none came. Peter stared at the tabletop without any indication that he wanted to cooperate. Patty signaled Rick and they stood up.

"We're going to talk next with Stuart. I wanted to talk with you first, Peter, because the first one to tell us what happened will have some leniency in their sentence. I wanted that opportunity to go to you. I'm sorry it won't. Goodbye, Peter."

Patty and Rick walked to the door and were about to leave when they heard Peter's voice.

"I wasn't on the boat. I was on the shore at Macklyn Cove. Max had told me to wait there."

Patty and Rick glanced at each other, walked back to the table, and sat down.

"Max said that he and Stuart and another guy were going diving for abalone. I waited on the shore for a long time. They left the harbor in Max's boat. I was told that they'd need me to help carry the abalone up to the car. The fog had rolled in, and I was shivering. But I was afraid to leave. Afraid of what Max would do to me if I did." Peter stopped talking and cleared his throat.

"Would you like some water?" Patty asked.

Peter nodded. Rick walked to the door, opened it, and asked the guard if he'd bring the prisoner a cup of water. Peter drank his water and continued.

"Finally, the fog began to clear about the same time I heard a boat engine. I looked out at Diver Rock and saw the boat."

Patty leaned forward. "You are doing well, Peter. Could you tell how many people were in the boat?"

"Not right away. But as the fog continued to clear and I could make out the shapes, I saw three people. Then it cleared enough that I recognized Max and Stuart, but I didn't know the third guy."

"You're doing great, Peter. What did you see next?"

Peter cocked his head to the side and squinted his eyes. "One of them sat up on the side of the boat, then fell over backwards into the water the way divers do."

Rick continued taking notes as Patty asked questions. "Could you see which one of the guys that was?"

"I really couldn't tell then, but I knew after learning about Jerry's death that the first guy in the water was Stuart."

"This is very important, Peter. Tell us every little detail about what you saw next."

"The fog continued to clear. I remember because it allowed the sun to shine, and I warmed up. I saw a second guy sit on the side of the boat and fall over backwards. No. That isn't all I saw. It appeared as though the guy inserted his mouthpiece after sitting on the edge of the boat. But then he quickly lifted his arm and pulled the mouthpiece out. I could see it in his hand. Then Max stood up and reached out at the guy. I couldn't tell what he was doing, but the guy fell over into the water."

"Peter, you are doing great. Will you do me a favor? Close your eyes and see the boat in your mind's eye. See the guy sitting on the edge of the boat. Tell me every detail about his and Max's movements. Take your time."

Peter closed his eyes. "The guy sits on the edge of the boat. I see him reach out to pick something up. I assume he picked up his mouthpiece because I see his arm bend and his elbow stick out. But almost immediately after putting his mouthpiece in, his hand and arm made a sweeping motion back up to the level of his mouth, and he pulled out his mouthpiece. Then Max reached out, and the guy fell backward into the water."

"Open your eyes, Peter. Now, close them again and see only what Max is doing. Was Max attempting to grab the diver or push him?"

Peter closed his eyes again and sat quietly. He picked his hand up and made the gesture he saw. "Max pushed the diver."

"Are you sure, Peter?"

"Yes. Max used both hands and pushed the guy at his shoulders."

Rick continued to take notes while Patty went on with the questions. "What did you see next?"

"I saw Max quickly sit on the side of the boat and lean over backward. He went into the water."

"How much time do you think passed between Max pushing the guy into the water and Max going in himself?"

Peter paused before answering. "It was fast. Maybe five seconds."

"So now, you've seen all three guys leave the boat and enter the water. What did you see next?"

"I continued to wait. I figured they'd be down about an hour because that's what I see most divers do out here. I don't remember exactly how long they were under, but I don't think it was a whole hour before I saw Stuart come up. He hung onto the side of the boat and threw his bag of abalone into it and climbed in. A second diver came up next. I didn't realize it at first, but it was Max. He handed his bag of abalone to Stuart, and then handed Stuart his vest and tank. Then he climbed into the boat. Then they just sat in the boat for what must have been about fifteen minutes.

"I kept expecting to see the other diver come up, but he didn't. That's when Max saw me on the beach and waved. I waved back and saw Stuart get into the water without his tank. Max handed him both bags of abalone, and Stuart started swimming toward the shore where I waited. When he came to shore, he handed one of the abalone bags to me and said that Max wanted me to go with him to Max's house. So I followed Stuart up the walkway to where his car was parked."

"Peter, was Max still in the boat when you walked to Stuart's car?"

Peter looked down at the table while he thought. "No. I remember Max going back into the water after he handed Stuart the two bags of abalone."

"And you didn't see Max's boat leave?"

"No, but I heard it. Stuart and I had started up the pathway to his car, and I heard the engine start up. Then I heard the boat leave. I turned and could no longer see the boat or Max."

"How can you be so sure that the boat you heard leave belonged to Max?"

"Because his was the only one out there. And I'd heard the engine when Max arrived. I'm sure it was Max's boat that left."

Rick stopped writing and looked up. "That's all very helpful, Peter. Did it cross your mind when you heard Max leave that he probably was leaving without the third diver?"

Peter's eyes teared up. "Yes. I knew Max was leaving without the diver, and I mentioned it to Stuart."

"What did Stuart say?"

"He told me that it was none of my business. He said, 'Max had something he needed to take care of.' And then Stuart told me to keep my mouth shut or Max would take care of me too. I didn't know for sure then that Max had killed the guy, but I did wonder. I knew that I couldn't go to the police or Max would hurt me."

"Where did you go with Stuart?"

"We went to Max's house where Stuart's also living. He and I cleaned the abalone. Then he put three on the counter for dinner and the rest in the freezer. When Max arrived, he prepared the three that Stuart didn't freeze, and the three of us ate them."

"Did Max say anything about the other diver?"

"He didn't talk about him at all. He just thanked me for helping and said it was only fair that he and Stuart share their catch with me. After a couple of hours, Max told Stuart to drive me home. Before I left, he grabbed me by the shoulders. Then he said, 'You know abalone diving is illegal, don't you, Peter?' I shrugged my shoulders and responded, 'I guess.' Then he said, 'You didn't see anything today, did you, Peter? You didn't see my boat or me or Stuart or anyone else. Right?' I was scared and told Max that I didn't see anything."

Rick made a few notes while Patty picked up the questioning. "And then you left with Stuart?"

Peter looked down at the top of the table. "No. That's when Max gave me the knife and sheath. I didn't know then that they had belonged to Jerry. Max told me that I was one of his friends now. Then he said, 'Don't ever make me mad at you, Peter, or I'll do to you what I did to Tim.'" Peter squeezed his eyes shut as though to stop the tears that had built up in them. "I'm sorry. I was just so scared. I knew then that Max had killed that diver, and I knew what he'd done to Tim. I had no doubt he'd kill me if I said anything about that day." Peter crossed his arms on the table and laid his head on top of his arms.

Patty looked at Rick and signaled that it was about time to wrap up the interview.

"Peter."

The young man looked up at Patty.

"We will see what we can do about commuting your sentence. I need to ask you something. You've gone a few weeks now without needing the drugs you were taking. Do you want to get help when you're let out so that you don't go back to using?"

Peter raised his head. "I'm never using again. If I need help, I'll get it. I don't ever want to end up in jail again, Detective O'Toole. Believe me, I plan to start living my life without fear."

Peter was returned to his cell, and the detectives started their drive back to Brookings.

Patty stared out the passenger window. "I'll talk with the DA tomorrow. See what we can do about helping Peter start life over."

CHAPTER TWENTY-FOUR

"I hope your intuition about Peter proves to be accurate. Now we've got a thirty-minute drive back to the office. So I've got a question and a request."

"Okay. What's your question?"

"Have you been to the Hawthorne Gallery in Port Orford?"

"As a matter of fact, I have, but it's been a while. Why do you ask?'

"I am planning our day outing, and I'd like to start off by driving to Port Orford and touring the gallery. We can then stop for brief hikes along the coast back to Brookings."

Patty smiled. "First, let me say that I'm impressed.   Second, I'd love to enjoy the gallery with you. I've been there several times, and both the gallery and the artwork are inspiring. The Redfish Restaurant is fabulous too, with its views of the ocean and Battle Rock. So, now that I've answered your question, what's your request?"

"I figure that you know so much about the area that you can tell me about the gallery while I'm driving. That will give me a greater appreciation of the art."

"Well, that's easy. The gallery in Port Orford is the Hawthornes' second. The first opened in Big Sur in 1995. You'll see art in several media that includes pieces by family members and friends. There are works in glass, clay, paint, and metal. Chris Hawthorne creates beautiful glass-blown jellyfish!"

"Well, if I hadn't already decided I wanted to start our outing there, I'd be putting it on my to-do list."

"While I'm playing tour guide, I might as well mention that Battle Rock was named for a real battle that took place in 1851 between the Qua-to-mah native Americans and William Tichenor's men."

"You really are a walking encyclopedia, Patty."

Patty laughed. "No, I just enjoy knowing about places I visit. The Oregon coast is rich with history. I have to say, Rick, that I'm really looking forward to this outing you're taking me on. It will be a lot of fun."

Rick smiled. "I hope so." He pulled into the police station parking lot. "Guess we'd better put our minds back on work. We've got enough from Peter to implicate Stuart in the murder of Jerry Stengle if Stuart knew Max's intent."

"Agreed," said Patty. "Let's bring him in again and let him know we have an eyewitness to his being on the boat with Max. Maybe we can convince him that by talking about Jerry's murder, he'll help himself when he admits to the murder of Max."

Rick looked at Patty. "If he did it. There's someone else we should visit again too."

"Who's that?"

"Tim's parents. I'd like to give them the news that Max is dead."

"Yeah, it would be better if we told them in person. I hope it brings them some peace."

Patty called Brad and asked him to bring Stuart back in as soon as possible. Brad was back on the phone with Patty in less than ten minutes.

"He'll be here in an hour. Said he'd already made up his mind to come in."

"That's great, Brad. Thanks."

Patty ended the call. "Brad says Stuart was intending on coming in. Maybe our talking about him being an accessory has him scared."

"That," Rick said, "or he's going to admit to the murder of Max."

"Wouldn't that be a prize? We'd be wrapping up two cases in as many days."

"I could use a snack," said Rick. "You want something?"

"A refill on my coffee would be great. Thanks."

Rick took Patty's mug and left the room. When he returned, Patty was on the phone.

"That's great, Mom. Did the sale bring in enough to cover your immediate HOA maintenance needs? I guess that means you'll need another sale or an assessment. Becky's doing fine, Mom. Whenever I call, she's either in class or studying. I'd like her to relax a little and take time to have some fun, but all she seems to focus on is getting good grades. And she does. I was? I don't remember studying all the time. I did? Well, maybe the reason I want her to have a little fun is because I didn't. Yeah, I have done okay, haven't I? I'm doing what I enjoy, and I'm good at it. My hope for Becky is that she'll experience the same thing after graduation. You too, Mom. Tell Bill I said, 'Hi.' I will. Bye."

Rick set down his coffee mug. "How's your mom today?"

"She's doing well. She said that the garage sale their homeowners' association held brought in about five thousand to go toward repairs."

Rick chuckled. "A garage sale brought in five thousand dollars? I had no idea a garage sale could produce anywhere near that much money."

"Yes, but she also said that the price tag on the repairs they need is about twenty thousand. She expects they'll each be given an assessment."

"I heard you mention Becky."

"Yeah. I was telling my mom about how hard Becky studies and how little fun she has. Mom said I was the same way."

Rick cocked his head and lifted his eyebrows. He changed the subject. "Oh. Stuart's coming in soon. How do you want to handle the interview?"

"My thought is that we first listen to what he has to say. If he doesn't come clean, we'll let him know we've got an eyewitness. If that doesn't start him talking, we can be good cop/bad cop."

"And, in that final act, you want me to be bad cop?"

Patty smiled. "Of course. You're particularly good in that role. Much better than I'd be."

CHAPTER TWENTY-FIVE

Stuart arrived at the police station as cocky as ever. Brad walked him down the hall to the interview room.

Patty and Rick walked in and sat down. Rick pulled a pen from his pocket and opened his file. Patty nodded to the young man slouching in his chair.

"Hello again, Stuart. Officer Bradley says that you wanted to come in and talk to us."

Stuart fidgeted. "That's right."

Patty waited for him to continue and then posed the obvious question. "We're here, Stuart. What would you like to tell us?"

"Before I start talking, I want you to promise that I won't do any jail time."

Patty shook her head. "You know it doesn't work that way, Stuart. You tell us what you know, and we'll say whether we can help you."

Stuart stayed quiet and then sat up. "Okay, if you're going to be like that, I've got nothing to say. No sense in my trying to help you out if you're not going to promise to help me." He stood up. "I'm leaving."

"Before you go, Stuart, Detective Starker and I do have something we'd like to say to you. Will you please take your seat again?"

Stuart turned around. "There's nothing you can say to me that's going to make me talk unless you promise to keep me out of jail."

Patty spoke softly. "We have an eyewitness."

Stuart froze. His skin color paled. "An eyewitness? To what?"

"Someone saw you, Max, and Jerry in the boat at Diver Rock. Now, come sit down."

Stuart slowly walked back to the table and sat down. He stared at the top of the table.

Patty and Rick remained silent.

Stuart looked up at Patty and then at Rick. "You're bluffing me. It was foggy. No one could have seen us."

Patty looked at Rick and then back to Stuart. "You remember the fog."

Stuart's eyes opened a little larger as he seemed to be trying to think.

Patty continued her soft approach. "What happened that day, Stuart? Why did you agree to participate with Max in a murder?"

Stuart suddenly found his voice. "I didn't have anything to do with murdering Jerry. I was in the boat, but I won't tell you anything else unless I know I won't go to jail."

"Tell us what you know, Stuart. Then we'll let you know whether we can help you."

"No. That's not what you told me last time. You said you'd see what you could do to help me if I talked."

"Stuart, look at me." Stuart looked into Patty's eyes. "The way things work is that the first person to give us information leading to a conviction of the responsible gets our help if we want to give it. But you passed on that earlier opportunity, Stuart. Like I said, we now have an eyewitness who saw it all. Now, if you can tell us something we don't already know, maybe we can offer some help."

Stuart slumped back into his chair and then sat up straight again. The cocky attitude was gone. He stumbled with his words. "I, I don't know what to do."

Patty gently put her hand on Stuart's arm. "Just talk to us. Why did you go with Max to Diver Rock when you knew he was going to murder Jerry?"

"I didn't know he was going to kill Jerry. Max told me that the three of us were going diving for abalone. He told me that Jerry was a friend from high school."

"But you were seen taking the abalone from Max and swimming to shore even though Jerry had not returned to the boat."

"I just thought Jerry was late. And Max said he'd go back in after him. After I took the abalone, Max put his tank on and went back into the water. I looked back and saw him fall over the side of the boat. I figured the worst thing that could happen would be we'd get caught with the abalone."

Patty sat back in her chair.

Rick leaned forward. "When did you know Max had killed Jerry?"

Stuart shook his head before responding. "Max had this other friend, Peter, who was on shore when I swam back with the abalone. Max told me in the boat that he'd asked his friend Peter to help me get the abalone to the car. He told me to bring Peter to the house with me."

Rick repeated his question. "And when did you know Max had killed Jerry?"

"Later that night. Max, Peter, and I ate some abalone and drank a couple beers. Then Max told me to take Peter home." Stuart paused and shook his head again. "Before Peter and I left, Max gave Peter a knife and sheath. I saw the name Stengle on the sheath and Jerry's initials on the knife. That's when I knew."

Rick continued. "So you knew then that Max had left Jerry back at Diver Rock. Not long after that day, we spoke with you about Jerry being missing. Why didn't you talk to us?"

Stuart looked at Rick and began to stiffen his upper body. "You didn't know Max. Everyone thought Max and I were best friends. Even Max called me his best friend. But I knew that if I crossed Max, he'd kill me before I could figure out where to run. The truth is I hated Max Rainy and all he stood for."

Patty spoke with a stern voice. If that's the case, Stuart, did you kill Max?'

Stuart slapped his hands on top of the table. "No! But I'd like to thank whoever did."

"You had opportunity, skill, and motive," said Rick. "You know how to operate a speargun. You've just admitted to hating him, and he involved you in his murder scheme. You've done nothing but lie to us since we first spoke with you. Why should we believe you now?"

"Because I'm not a murderer. And I was too scared to even think about killing Max for fear he'd read my thoughts."

"Tell us about Connor and Trevor. What part did they play in Jerry's murder?"

Stuart shook his head. "I don't know what they've told you, but Max and I didn't see them much. They didn't hang out with us, and I don't think Max would have told anyone about the abalone dives. That is, unless he was sure they wouldn't go to the cops. Peter, Jerry, and I were the only ones who knew about the abalone dives."

"You've mentioned dives," said Rick. "I saw the abalone in the freezer at Max's house and in his mother's home. How many dives were there?"

Stuart shrugged his shoulders. "I don't know. Maybe six or seven. Max would just get up one day and tell me to get my gear."

Rick closed his file and stood up. Patty walked to the door, opened it, and spoke with Brad. Officer Bradley took out his handcuffs and walked toward Stuart while Patty began reciting his rights.

"You have the right to remain silent…"

Stuart backed away. "Wait a minute. I told you what you wanted to know. So why are you arresting me?"

Patty and Rick walked out of the room, and Officer Chekowski stepped in to assist Brad with Stuart.

The detectives filled their coffee mugs, returned to their desks, and checked phone messages.

"I've got a message from Doc Miller," said Patty. She hit the doc's number on speed-dial.

"Detective O'Toole. Thanks for getting back to me."

"Sure, Doc. I would have called back sooner, but Rick and I were interviewing a person of interest associated with Jerry Stengle's murder."

"Did the interview help?"

"It did, Doc. It was our second one today, and together they provide more than enough circumstantial evidence against Max Rainy."

"Well, Detective. You can now do better than that. The unknown liquid you found in the syringes in Max's garage is succinylcholine. The chance of Rainy having this drug in his home and not being the killer is practically nil. However, someone could argue that he may have kept the drug for some reason unknown to anyone else. That argument is substantially diluted when one learns that the syringe found in his late mother's medicine cabinet also has traces of succinylcholine."

"Thanks, Doc. That's great news! The lab's findings help us tie up one, probably two murders, but our killer won't be tried and convicted for the murders he committed or for the injuries inflicted upon Timothy Rollins."

"You have a point, Patty. Though I've learned that families of the victims receive some sort of satisfaction from watching the responsible suffer through a trial and incarceration, I'm just grateful Max Rainy is no longer able to maim and kill."

"I hear you, Doc, and I agree."

"Before you go, Patty, I have an additional lab result that will not ease your work burden."

"Is this about Max's speargun?"

"It is. The only fingerprints found on it and the spear are those of Max Rainy."

"Rick and I expected that would be the case."

"Tell Rick I said congratulations to you both for solving the Stengle murder."

"Your words are appreciated, Doc. I'll let Rick know."

The call ended, and Patty went over the doc's findings with Rick. "I should let the lieutenant know. I'll tell him about our interview with Stuart too. Maybe he'll have an opinion about Stuart's innocence or guilt."

"I'll start a list," said Rick, "of possible suspects and their reasons for wanting Max dead."

In her meeting with the lieutenant, Patty explained the fear Stuart expressed about Max. "What are your thoughts on Stuart's innocence, LT?"

The lieutenant listened, and when Patty was done talking, he sat back in his chair. "Let's start first with Max Rainy. He was a textbook psychopath. A man without a conscience who had no regard for others. A psychopath sees people as objects to use for their own benefit.

"Psychopaths don't always murder. Some use manipulation and reckless behavior to achieve their goals. It seems Rainy exhibited all these traits. He was calculating, plotting, and did whatever it took to get his way."

Patty nodded and continued to listen.

"Now, about Stuart. He said he didn't know that Max was going to kill Jerry. That he'd left the boat thinking Max had re-entered the water intending to find Jerry. Your witness, Peter, seemed to describe the same actions as he watched from the shore. Stuart said he didn't comprehend that Max had killed Jerry until he saw the knife and sheath. With no proof otherwise, I think a jury would agree with Stuart.

"So did he kill Max Rainy? Well, it's possible. We know from Stuart and Peter's descriptions of Max, and the manipulating fear he hung over them, that Stuart's need for revenge could have become greater than his fear of being killed. But there's nothing in his character that suggests he could murder. Having said that, it doesn't eliminate the possibility that something happened between Max and Stuart that caused Stuart to snap. It means finding Rainy's killer isn't going to be easy for you and Rick."

Patty exhaled loudly. "Thanks for your insight, LT. I'll go over this with Rick, and we'll keep working on it. One last question, LT. Do you think Rosemary Rainy's body should be exhumed?"

The lieutenant repeated the question. "Should Rosemary Rainy's body be exhumed? Practically speaking, after three years we won't find evidence of an injection site or the succinylcholine. You don't need additional evidence to convict the assumed responsible since he's dead. Does Rosemary Rainy have living relatives other than Max who might want to know whether she was murdered by her son?"

"None that we know of," said Patty.

"Then my answer to your question is 'no.' The syringe found in Mrs. Rainy's bathroom medicine cabinet should be logged into the evidence room for future use, if needed."

Patty sat quietly taking in what her lieutenant had explained and his opinions deduced from the known facts.

"Does that sit okay with you, Detective O'Toole?"

"Yes, LT. It does. Thanks again."

Patty walked back to her desk and filled Rick in on her conversation with the lieutenant.

"Did you make your list?

"I did."

"This a good time to go over it?"

"It is."

"Good. Let's go over the list, and then I'll call Randy Stengle and schedule a time for us to stop by. I'd like to inform him in person about the confirmation of Max being his brother's murderer. The meeting may help us to form an opinion on whether he should be on our list of suspects."

Rick put the list in front of him. "Stuart is at the top of the list, though given the lieutenant's comments, he's not as strong a suspect as we might previously have thought."

Patty started to make notes. "Still, like the LT said, he could have snapped. We know from earlier conversations that he's a skilled liar."

"Let's come back to Stuart," said Rick. "The second name I wrote down is Randy's. He was pretty close to his brother and would have motive."

Patty tapped the end of her pen on the desk. "We had not yet found the succinylcholine when Max was killed. What reason would he have to murder Max before we had proof?"

"I don't know, but he may know enough about Max's behavior to have believed it was him based upon the circumstances around his brother's disappearance and death. We need to question him."

"I agree. What about Connor and Trevor?"

Rick sat back in his chair. "I don't see either one of them for it, but it might be good to question them again now that Max is no longer a threat."

"That's pretty much all we've got," said Patty. "Peter was locked up, and Tim no longer lives here."

"He doesn't, but he could have killed Max and left again without anyone knowing. He certainly had motive. We don't know the extent of his injuries other than the loss of one eye, so it's questionable as to whether he has the means to have committed the murder himself."

"Unless," said Patty, "he hired someone to do the job."

"That's a possibility," said Rick. "His parents didn't know where he lived when we met with him, and I doubt they'd tell us even if they did. Let's run him through the system. See if he has any priors."

Patty picked up the phone. "I'll ask Brad to take care of that."

"While you talk with Brad, I'll schedule time with Randy Stengle. Okay with you if I schedule the interview after lunch?" Patty nodded.

After completing their respective phone calls, Rick stood up. "My stomach's going to start growling any minute now. So, to spare me any embarrassment, let's go eat."

Twenty minutes later, Rick was enjoying a ham and Swiss sandwich with fries while Patty worked on a Cobb salad. They'd barely started their meal when a woman approached Rick.

"Excuse me."

Rick looked up with his mouth full. The woman noticed his inability to politely respond and continued to talk. "I noticed the badge hooked on your belt. You're a policeman, right?"

With his mouth still full, Rick nodded.

"Well, I don't mean to interrupt your lunch, but I wonder if you can help me."

Rick glanced at Patty, and she responded to the woman. "We're detectives, ma'am. What do you need?"

The woman smiled at Patty. "Oh, you're with the police too. Well, that's good. Maybe one of you can help me. I live a few blocks from here in a small house. Well, not too small, but it's big enough for me and Sam. Sam doesn't really need too much room. Anyway, I have a big yard. Well, not really big, you know, but it's a nice size for Sam and me. I have neighbors, and they have yards too. I have a fence around my back yard. I had to put up a fence to keep out the deer."

Rick continued to eat while the woman spoke. Patty poked at her salad.

"Before I had the fence I couldn't plant anything without the deer eating it. One year they ate all of my lettuce and roses."

Patty spoke quickly and gently while the woman took a breath. "Is there a police matter you need help with, ma'am?"

"Oh, yes. There is. It's about my neighbor and his cat. You see, my Sam is a cat, and I take good care of him. I buy him the best cat food, and I have a litter box in our house for him. I put a long leash on Sam when I let him out of the house so that he can't jump the fence and go into the neighbor's yard, but it's long enough so that he can explore. And I take care of our yard. I enjoy my vegetable and flower gardens."

The waitress arrived and cleared Rick's dishes.

Patty asked for a box. She looked up at the woman. "We need to get back to work, ma'am. There is a sheriff's substation just down the hill from here at the port. Maybe you could stop in there and talk with one of the friendly volunteers at the front desk."

The woman looked confused. "Well, I'm almost done, and I'd hate to have to tell the whole story all over again. You see, my problem is my neighbor's cat. He lets it out in the morning and doesn't take it back in until dark. So the cat is out all day. And that means it doesn't use a litter box. So it's using my yard. I've talked to my neighbor, but he says it's my problem. I don't know what to do. Can you help me?"

Rick brought the palms of his hands up as though pushing something toward Patty, gesturing to let him answer the woman's question. "There's a motion-response sprinkler you can attach to your hose and point across your yard. When the cat comes over, the sprinkler shoots a spray of water. It will keep the cats off your lawn."

The woman smiled. "Oh, that will be wonderful. Do you know where I can buy one?"

"Try Cascade Home Center or Gold Beach Lumber. If they don't have one, ask someone who works there to go online and find one for you."

"Oh, thank you, Detective. You've been a great help. I'm so glad I stopped to speak to you. Thanks again."

The woman left and the detectives paid their bill. Patty stood up with her boxed salad.

"Well, gee, that was certainly nice of you to listen to that woman's story before giving her a solution to her problem."

Rick shrugged. "No problem."

Patty laughed. "Where did you learn about the sprinkler?"

"I have a friend whose been using one for years to keep deer out of his yard."

CHAPTER TWENTY-SIX

Patty sat down and set her folder on the table. "Hello, Randy. We appreciate your meeting with us again."

"Sure. No problem. You said on the phone that you had something to tell me about my brother's death."

Patty nodded. "We do, Randy. What I'm about to tell you will be difficult. Rick and I searched Max Rainy's house and found evidence that he murdered your brother."

Randy showed no facial reaction to the news. His hands told a different story as they clenched into fists. "What kind of evidence?"

"Syringes full of a drug called succinylcholine and peanut oil."

"How were the oil and drug used?"

"Max put the peanut oil on Jerry's mouthpiece. That would have put your brother in anaphylactic shock. Max pushed him over the side of the boat and then injected the drug between Jerry's fingers, paralyzing him."

Randy's forehead now showed lines of stress as he reacted to the manner in which his brother had been killed. "How long does it take to drown?"

Patty glanced at Rick and turned back to Randy. "Your brother would have died within seconds."

Randy got up out of his chair and walked across the room.

Patty and Rick waited until the young man was prepared to go on. Patty noticed tears in his eyes when he joined the detectives again at the table.

"Do you have any suspects for Max's murder?"

"Not yet," said Patty. "Do you know of anyone who hated Max bad enough to kill him?"

Randy looked at Patty and Rick. His next words were spoken in anger. "Well, me for one."

Patty and Rick stared at Randy as he continued.

"I didn't want Jerry diving with Max because Jerry wasn't certified. And he told me Max was strange but that he could handle himself. Yeah, I was angry enough to want Max dead."

Rick opened his file and set a photo in front of Randy. Randy looked down at the photo of Max lying on the floor with a spear through his chest. Patty and Rick both watched for Randy's reaction. When none came, Rick continued.

"You told us that you didn't know how to dive. But you must have been around the equipment since Jerry was a diver. Could you handle a speargun?"

Randy stared at the photo and then at Rick. "Are you asking me if I killed Max? I wish I had. I wish I had the ability to face him, release the spear, and watch him die. I could have told him that I was doing it for my brother. No, I didn't kill Max Rainy. It took someone who despised him as much as I did and had the courage to do what needed to be done. It wasn't me, and you're looking for someone with a lot less fear than I have."

"If it wasn't you, then help us out," said Patty. "Who else do you know who also knew Max?"

"I probably know some of the guys from school who knew Max and Randy. I remember Tim, but they were all a couple years older than me."

"What can you tell us about Tim?"

"Only that he seemed like a nice guy. His parents were always trying to help Jerry and me after Mom and Dad died. But, like I told you before, life was a mess for us after our folks were killed. Then Jerry had his accident. I was trying to help Jerry from becoming unhinged. Life was a nightmare for what seemed like a long, long time.

"I'm sorry, but I really don't know anyone who knew Max and would have killed him."

Rick put the photo back in his file.

Patty stood up. "Thanks for your help," she said. "There may be a counselor in Brookings who can see you if you find yourself needing to talk with someone. Give me a call if you'd like help. I'm sure the counselor will work something out with you."

"Thanks, but that won't be necessary. My life has been about loss for as long as I can remember. I just have to accept it."

"There's no shame in seeking help, Randy. You've experienced more loss during your young life than most people two and three times your age. Give yourself some slack."

Randy walked the detectives to the front door.

"Thanks for telling me about Max. It helps to know it was him for sure. And it helps that he's no longer around to hurt someone else."

Patty and Rick were quiet on the drive back to Brookings. As they walked into their office, Patty's cell phone rang. "Detective O'Toole."

"Hello, Detective O'Toole. This is your mother."

"Hi, Mom. How's your day going?"

"It's been fairly good, Patty. Do you have time to talk?"

"I do, Mom. What's up?"

"I just thought I'd share a little more about Grace. She and I had lunch today."

"Lunch sounds nice, Mom."

"It was, Patty. And Grace told me more about her life. Her mother was mentally ill. Today we know the condition as bipolar disorder, but when Grace was a child they just referred to her mother as being odd and sick. Grace remembers times when her mother was happy and excited about everything. She'd talk about plans for the family to travel around the world. Grace says she knew her mom's ideas were not realistic, but she loved seeing her mom happy. Then, without warning, her mother would be unable to get out of bed in the morning. She might spend weeks hiding in the house without getting out of her nightgown and robe. At those times, Grace said, keeping up the house was up to her since her mother was unable to cope. Isn't it sad, Patty?"

"It is sad, Mom. Today we have medications that can allow those afflicted with bipolar to live a normal life. I cannot imagine a child growing up with a parent that ill, but Grace seems to have been able to pull together the strength to do so. Was her father helpful?"

"I asked Grace about her father. She said he worked long days and kind of ignored her mother's mood swings. She says he never talked with her about her mother being ill. Grace thinks her father probably worked long hours to keep from becoming deeply depressed."

"Well, Mom, from what you've shared with me, Grace is a lovely woman who is lucky to have such a good friend in you. I'm sure you brighten her days as, it seems, she brightens yours."

"Grace told me today that these later years in life have been her best, and she really enjoys our time together. I told her I enjoyed my visits with her too. To be truthful, Patty, knowing Grace enriches my life."

"I think you and Grace have each found a true friend in the other. I hope to meet her someday."

"Oh, you will. I'll be getting in touch soon with some options for an evening when you and Becky can come to dinner and meet Grace. Rick too, if that's okay with you. Bill has already met her."

"Sounds good, Mom, and inviting Rick is more than okay with me. I look forward to us all getting together and meeting Grace. Hope your day continues to go well."

"Yours too, dear."

Rick was drinking coffee and reading a file when Patty ended the call with her mom. She fidgeted in her chair to get Rick's attention. "I'm looking forward to our adventure tomorrow. When and where should we meet?"

Rick closed the file in front of him. "I'll pick you up. The weather predictions are in the high sixties. We'll drive up the coast to Port Orford, enjoying the spectacular ocean views along the way. When we're replete with viewing beautiful art, we'll start back to Brookings, stopping along the way to hike some of our ocean-side trails. At some point during mid-day, we'll eat lunch. Sound okay?"

Patty smiled. "I'm going to love it!"

Patty and Rick locked eyes. "Me too," he said.

CHAPTER TWENTY-SEVEN

Rick picked Patty up at nine. "The weather came through as predicted."

Patty smiled. "I agree. Nice of you to put in the order."

Rick opened the passenger door, and Patty climbed up into his pickup. "This is the first time I've been in your truck. It's comfortable."

"Yeah. I like it. A pickup is a necessity when you have a house that needs work and a few acres of land."

Patty raised her eyebrows. "I've seen your house. Do you have another one that I don't know about?"

"Not yet. But I've been looking at land, and when I see what I want, I'm going to buy it."

"That's great. I know that owning land is important to you."

"I just need some distance between me and my neighbors. The place I have now is a nice little house, but there's too much noise."

"Oh, are they fighting or playing loud music?"

"No need for anyone to yell for me to hear them. A normal conversation in their backyard can be heard in my house if the window's open. That's too close for me. It isn't that they're not nice people, it's just that I'm handling problems with people all day and I want to have my own space to go home to in the evening." Rick paused and glanced at Patty. "Can you understand that?"

"I do, Rick, and I understand the desire to own land. I've always thought it would be great to have enough land for a few animals and a large garden. It's just more than I could have ever handled on my own with Becky. I hope that you find what you're looking for."

"Thanks, Patty. Do you ever think about your future once Becky's graduated and on her own?"

Patty laughed. "Frequently. I've got Mom to think about, and I know that she and Bill will need more care as they age. I can't imagine working anyplace else, so I've always planned to remain in Brookings. Since I've accepted the idea of working until retirement age, I've still got a way to go. Then I'll figure out how to fill my free time. Curry County has lots of volunteer activities."

"If things in your life changed, do you think you could adjust to a new way of living?"

Patty turned and looked at Rick. "Changed? How?"

Rick stared out of his window. "Oh, I don't know. What if you won the lottery?"

Patty laughed again. "Yes, I suppose I would make a few changes if I won the lottery. But don't ask me what those would be because, right now, I have no idea. The thing is, Rick, I'm not unhappy with my life. My divorce from Becky's dad left me with a lot of pain and broken dreams, but I got through the toughest years, and with Mom's help, raised Becky to be a smart, self-assured young lady. That makes me incredibly happy. I was raised with the understanding that life isn't fair and often is downright cruel. But it's a journey. You take what each day gives you and try to make the most of it."

"That's a good way to look at life. No wonder you're such a great detective."

"Wow, Rick. I don't think you've ever told me that. This day is getting better all the time, and we've only just started out."

Rick looked at Patty, caught her eye, and smiled.

The day proceeded as planned. The detectives toured the Hawthorne Gallery and admired the view from the Redfish Restaurant. They headed down the coast to hike on one or more of the coastline trails.

"It's eleven thirty," said Rick. "How about we enjoy lunch at our next stop?"

"Sounds like a good idea to me. I'm hungry."

At the chosen site, Rick opened his backpack and pulled out sandwiches, chips, pickles, potato salad, and a couple bottles of Perrier. He handed Patty a plastic cup and poured. He poured himself a cup and held it up for a cheer.

"To the best partner a detective could ask for. One who is also my best friend."

They tapped their cups together and sipped.

"Thank you for that toast, Rick. I just want to add that you, too, are the best partner and friend I could ask for. And I'm very, very happy you returned to Brookings."

The detectives continued to enjoy their lunch.

"Have you noticed the sea stars?" asked Patty. "They're returning."

"I have noticed," said Rick. "I wanted to know more about why the abalone harvesting has remained closed, and I found information about the relationship between the abalone and the sea stars. Do you know about the devastating disease that killed many of the sea stars in 2013 and 2014?"

"No, other than that the disappearance of some sea stars affected the entire ecosystem. What did you read?"

"The disease, which is still a mystery to scientists, affected at least twenty species of sea stars. Historically, there was a similar die-off in the nineteen-seventies, eighties, and nineties, but none of those were of the magnitude of the one a few years ago. The disease causes lesions to appear on the sea star, fol-lowed by decay of tissue around the lesions. Fragmentation of the body then occurs. The entire process can take place within a three-day period.

"The significant signs of recovery have been with the Ochre Sea Star. That's the one found on our coast. The sea star hit the hardest is the Sunflower. It's a massive sea star with sixteen or more limbs and a three-foot arm span. The Sunflower is the primary predator of sea urchins, which, due to the sea star die-off, have invaded the ocean floor in droves and eaten a great amount of kelp. Abalone eat kelp, therefore their numbers have been reduced with reduc-tion of the kelp forests.

"The harbor seals off the Brookings shore are also much fewer in number than in prior years. They eat fish, crustaceans, and mollusks that live in kelp forests. I expect they've found kelp forests elsewhere. Due to the reduction in abalone, the season shut down in 2018 and hasn't opened up again."

"I'd wondered," said Patty, "why there are so few harbor seals compared to a few years ago. I hope it won't be long before our kelp forests become dense again, allowing for a healthy abalone population and an increase in harbor seals."

The conversation paused. Both Rick and Patty quickly became aware of the silence between them. They looked at each other. Suddenly a nearby dog barked, interrupting the moment. Patty picked up half of her sandwich.

"This looks delicious."

A couple hours later, Rick pulled into Patty's driveway. He got out of the truck, walked around to Patty's door, and opened it for her. They walked to the front door.

Patty looked at Rick. "Do you want to come in for coffee?"

Rick stared into her eyes. "No. Not today. I think I'll head home."

"Okay. I had a wonderful time, Rick. This has been a fabulous day." Patty turned and unlocked the door.

"Patty?" She turned around, and Rick took her head between his hands. He leaned down and kissed her. "I hope to have lots more days like this with you." He turned and walked to his truck.

CHAPTER TWENTY-EIGHT

"I've reached Connor on his cell phone," said Rick. "He and Trevor will be fishing the mouth of the Chetco this afternoon. Might be a good time to talk with them."

"That works, Rick. I'm hoping one or both of them will talk more about Max now that there's no reason to fear him. Maybe they'll give us the name of someone we've not yet spoken with."

"Someone like Max," said Rick, "doesn't wake up one morning and become as violent and cunning as he was. That kind of a person has often left a trail of mayhem. There are others out there who had a death wish for Max. We just need to find the one who carried it out."

He put his coffee mug down. "If you're ready, we can head down to the port. I told Connor we'd see them about two."

"Sure. Let's go."

A few minutes later, Rick parked next to the river at the port RV park. He pointed toward a couple of guys fishing. "They're over there."

"How's the fishing?" asked Patty when they reached the men.

Connor nodded toward an empty bucket. "Not good."

Patty continued. "When's the last time either of you saw Max Rainy?"

The two guys looked at each other. Trevor turned back toward the river. Connor responded to Patty. "We haven't seen him since the last time we spoke with you. And since he's dead, there's no way we could have seen him over the past couple of days."

Patty glanced at Rick and then continued speaking with Connor. "How'd you hear?"

"Word travels fast through the fishing and diving circuit. I don't remember when or who told me. I just heard."

"Where were you yesterday morning?"

"We were hanging out at the dock. Unlike a lot of people, I had no reason to kill Max. He was a jerk, but I kept my distance."

"Know anyone who hated him enough to kill him?"

Trevor broke into a wide grin. Connor laughed and said, "I'll bet you've been laughed at before with that question."

Patty nodded. "I still need an answer."

"I know a few people who hated Max enough to kill him, but no one who'd have actually done the deed."

Rick spoke to Trevor. "What about you, Trevor? Where were you yesterday morning?"

"With Connor on the dock. We've got several people who can confirm that. I don't care at all that Max Rainy is dead. And I'd have such admiration for anyone who would kill Max that I'd never give him up to you."

The detectives glanced at each other. Patty nodded.

"Okay. Good luck with your fishing."

Connor responded without looking up. "No problem, Detectives."

CHAPTER TWENTY-NINE

Patty and Rick both arrived at the office early the next day. Patty brought bakery goods in a small white bag.

"I'll get the coffees," said Rick. He filled their cups and returned to his desk.

"We should be able to enjoy our first cup," said Patty. "Our only appointment today is with Mr. and Mrs. Rollins. She said we could come by about ten because by then Frank will have been able to shower and dress."

Rick swallowed his first bite of pastry. "That gives us a little time before leaving for Cave Junction. Let's discuss where we are on the case. We've gone through our list of persons of interest, and though they all celebrate Max's death, none said they could have carried it out. And I believe them."

Patty exhaled loudly and looked toward the window. "I do too. This will go down as our first cold case. My only comfort is that it's a cold case due to our not finding the murderer of a cold-blooded killer. I think I can live with that."

"I can," said Rick. "At least for now."

Patty looked from the window to Rick. "We'll be able to tell Mr. and Mrs. Rollins that the man who permanently disabled their son has died. Do you think the news will bring them both some peace?"

"Yeah, I do," said Rick.

"Then I'm going to believe that," said Patty. "Our jobs are full of so much sadness that it will be good to provide someone with helpful information."

* * *

Neither Rick nor Patty spoke much on the ride to the Rollins' home. Mrs. Rollins met them at the door.

"Come in, Detectives. My husband is waiting at the kitchen table."

Patty and Rick followed Mrs. Rollins into the kitchen and sat down at the table.

"Would you like tea or coffee?"

"No, thank you," said Patty. "We won't be here long."

Before Patty could continue, Mrs. Rollins began speaking.

"We were a happy family once. I want you to know that." The woman seemed to age as she spoke. Her uncombed hair suggested she hadn't taken time or didn't think to take the time to prepare herself for company. Her eyes were red and presented a look of sadness.

"When Frank and I married, we had planned to have several children. After three years, I went to the doctor because we figured something was wrong. I was put through a series of hormonal treatments and finally became pregnant.

"The result of that pregnancy was Timothy. He opened up a world to Frank and me that we'd previously accepted as something we'd never know. He was a perfect baby. Life took on new meaning for Frank and me. Frank worked hard to support his family, and I stayed home to care for our Tim. He was a good lad throughout his school years, and we enjoyed participating in activities with him and his friends."

Patty looked at Rick to communicate the need for them to stay with the Rollins until they'd had a chance to take in the news. She would eventually find some solace in knowing her son Timothy would never again have to fear the man who crippled him.

Mrs. Rollins continued. "When the accident happened and Max's sister was killed, everything changed. Max and Jerry and Tim were no longer young children. They were men, and near an age when some go off to war. When I'd ask Tim how school went, he'd shake his head and retreat to his room. Frank would attempt to get Tim to work out in the shed with him, but Tim had no interest. We realized, years later, that Tim just didn't want to discuss how much of a monster Max had become. He'd been friends with Max when they were younger, but within a few years their relationship changed. Max teased him mercilessly every chance he got. That's when Tim began losing his self-esteem. I believe he was afraid of Max. It seemed that it wasn't long after that, maybe a few years, that Max attacked Timothy."

Frank's hand bumped his coffee cup hard enough to make the hot liquid spill out. His hands shook, and he placed them in his lap. Tears formed in his eyes.

Patty took hold of Mrs. Rollins' hands that were tightly held together. "You don't have to tell us, Mrs. Rollins. Detective Starker and I are deeply sorry for all that you, Mr. Rollins, and Timothy have been through. We don't need convincing that Max Rainy was a monster and that his death is a blessing to you and your family."

After a quiet moment, Mrs. Rollins looked up at Patty. Her face was drawn, and tears welled up in her eyes before escaping down the deep lines etched into her face by excruciating pain. She removed her hands from under Patty's and placed them on top of those of her husband. Her tears had now stopped, and her voice became stronger.

"Our Timothy was in his early twenties when Max attacked him. Tim spent six months in and out of the hospital with a body so broken that none of the medical personnel expected him to live. He finally healed up enough to go home but required a walker to get around and could only see out of one eye. He was in constant pain." She looked up at the detectives. "You cannot imagine what it does to a parent's mind to know that the person who crippled and nearly killed your child was not punished and is now getting away with murdering someone else's child. The pain is such that only one familiar with insanity would understand."

Patty sat quietly, unable to take in anymore.

Rick looked over at Mr. Rollins and placed a hand on his shoulder. The old man's eyes had teared up as he stared down at the table while his wife spoke.

"Mr. Rollins," asked Rick, "did you kill Max Rainy?"

Mr. Rollins lifted his head, put the palms of his hands down on top of the table, and pushed himself to sit up straight.

"I did."

"How did you get into his place?"

"Tim rented a room from Max a few years ago. The key was still here."

Patty looked at Rick and then at Mrs. Rollins. They all sat silent, each taking in all that had been discussed.

Rick spoke again, breaking the silence.

"Frank Rollins, it pains me to have to do this."

"Before you go on," said Mrs. Rollins, "there's one more piece of information you need to have. The night before Frank killed Max we received a call. Our Timothy has died. He took his own life."

Rick sat back in his chair. He looked at his senior detective for direction. Mrs. Rollins still had her hands folded across those of her husband.

Patty looked at Rick and then toward the broken couple sitting silently at the table.

"We'll need to take Frank into the station. He'll be charged with the murder of Max Rainy. These are the actions we are under oath to take. But please understand that we will do everything we can, including testifying, to allow Frank to remain at home."

CHAPTER THIRTY

The sky was clear, and the sun reflected off the water, making it sparkle, creating the illusion of a blanket of diamonds. Waves gently lapped at the seashore. A few harbor seals lay sunning themselves on pieces of giant sea stacks that had separated from the mainland millions of years prior.

Patty and Rick sat on a rocky knoll watching an osprey. It dove several times straight down into the water, hitting feet first. One such dive rewarded the bird with a fish. It rose clumsily, with the fish face-forward in its talons. A couple of seagulls began chasing the osprey but failed to relieve the seabird of its catch.

Patty stared across the ocean. "I'm very happy, Rick."

"Yeah, it doesn't get much better than this, Patty."

Patty looked at Rick and smiled. "Doesn't get much better. What would make our time together perfect for you?"

"I have a response to that question, but I'd like to move a little closer and kiss you first."

Rick dug his foot into the loose dirt and pushed himself closer to Patty. He put his hand around her back.

Patty's gaze migrated from Rick's eyes to the dirt Rick's foot had just moved.

"Rick?"

"Don't say anything, Patty."

Patty pointed. "I think we've got a problem."

Rick looked to where Patty pointed. There, partially exposed, were the fingers of a human hand.

Fans of Detectives O'Toole and Starker are appreciated, and
for them I write a Murder, Mystery, & Suspense newsletter. To
receive the newsletter, log onto www.colorandwordsbygeorgia.com,
click on Contact Me and request to be added to my newsletter list.

G. A. Cockerham lives on the southern Oregon coast, the area of inspiration for her O'Toole/Starker murder mystery series. She is a retired financial advisor and insurance broker.